Dancer with Bruised Knees

Lynne McFall

Dancer with Bruised Knees

CHRONICLE BOOKS

SAN FRANCISCO

First paperback printing: April 1996.

"The Second Coming" by W. B. Yeats. Reprinted with permission of Macmillan Publishing Company from *The Poems of W. B. Yeats: A New Edition,* edited by Richard J. Finnerad. Copyright ©1924 by Macmillan Publishing Company, renewed ©1952 by Bertha Georgie Yeats.

The letter on pages 84–85 © by Robert G. Schuessler III. Used by permission.

Parts of this novel have appeared in slightly different form in *Story* magazine.

Library of Congress Cataloguing-in-Publication Data:
McFall, Lynne, 1948–
    Dancer with bruised knees / Lynne McFall.
    216 p. 14 x 20.3 cm.
    ISBN 0-8118-1259-6
    1. Women—United States—Fiction. I. Title.
PS3563.C3627D36   1994
813'.54—dc20   94-2088
                    CIP

Designed by Laura Lovett
Composition by On Line Type
Cover photograph copyright ©1996 by Jeff Hurwitz
Printed in the United States

Distributed in Canada by Raincoast Books,
8680 Cambie Street, Vancouver, B.C. V6P 6M9

10 9 8 7 6 5 4 3 2 1

Chronicle Books
275 Fifth Street
San Francisco, CA 94103

For my sister Sharon, my brother Monte,
my mother Louise, and my father Lucky.

෨

Souls for a day, here you must begin another cycle of mortal life which ends in death. No divinity shall cast lots for you; you must choose your own deity.

Plato, *Republic*

IT HAPPENED IN MY FORTIETH
year that I fell into a depression so deep that even the thought of sex could not raise me from it. I began, during this year of which I am going to speak, to doubt everything I had believed and had built my life on.

This is me, before the revolution. I am wearing a red dress, borrowed for the occasion, New Year's Eve. Though you can't tell it by looking, there is high color in my cheeks, the last of the fever. The prominence of the collar bones suggests a loss of weight, the eyes a period of melancholy. This is the only family resemblance I can see—this sorrow in the eyes. Otherwise I'm nothing like them.

My name is Sarah Blight. Except for the time I was married, I have lived on this land most of my life and should have left for good long ago. Every time I did leave there was a reason to come home. Now that there's no choice I am stupid with grief. Out of perversity or love, I don't know. This is my way of finding out.

My father taught me that photographs can show you something you didn't know you saw—like those drawings with the face hidden in the hump of a camel, the hag in the cape of a young woman. But here there's no trick. It's a picture of the world, not something imagined, something that could be faked. Though I've read that Diane

Arbus would raise her fist to get an expression she liked. There is that element of risk. And yet of a photograph I've heard it said, "This is my friend." It's that close to real.

This is my great grandmother, Victoria Blight, the person from whom I got my red hair. She is dancing at the edge of the abyss in Yosemite National Park, one leg flung up so high it threatens her ear, her arms raised in jubilation, her skirts flying. The expression on her face is unclear, though I imagine it to be one of ecstasy or defiance or abject terror, depending on my mood at the time. Did she know in the picture that she would die later that day? Was the decision her own, or something ineluctable, like a cat thrown down a dry well chooses a broken neck? I search the place where her eyes must be, hidden by the brim of her Dick Tracy hat. This is the picture that comes closest to the form of a question.

This is my grandmother, Shannon Marie Blight, Victoria's only daughter. Since the age of nineteen she has been a Christian Scientist, though she has Alzheimer's now and cannot remember this. All that's left of the person I loved are a few old sayings: "It's a great life if you don't weaken" and "T'ain't funny, McGee" and "Trust God but keep your powder dry." That's gunpowder.

Grandfather Blight was a railroad man, addicted to gambling and Mezcal, straight. That's him with the high-top shoes that look like spats. My grandmother would bring him a shot of tequila in bed every morning to jump-start his brain. The only thing I remember him saying is "Save the worm for me." At the end he played poker every night of the week, studying the red, white, and blue plastic chips as if they might provide some clue to his fate (and perhaps they did: the note he left was a list of pluses and minuses, with a minus-seven circled in red). His last act as an engineer was on a train traveling from Los Angeles to Blythe. Miles out into the Mojave, he spotted a lone car parked sideways across the tracks. Inside the car was a tramp. There was no possibility of avoiding a crash; the only question was how hard they would hit, how many would die. He didn't slow down, he said, because that would have increased the chances of being derailed—more passengers hurt, probably dead—and the result was that one tramp died who would have died anyway.

"Add it up," he said at the hearing. "More alive, less hurt. To slow down would have been suicide." He was involuntarily retired. Grandmother Blight said he was a man of principle, only it was the wrong principle.

I was raised an atheist with a sympathy for religious ritual. Candles and confessions, prayers and singing. My mother taught me that God is what we call the illusions we can't give up. Someone who listens when nobody's home. All-knowing Father (at this she snickered). Dispenser of cosmic justice (meaning, some dumb bastard who backs his pickup into your Maserati getting sideswiped shortly thereafter). Grandmother Blight, on the other hand, would have us read The Daily Lesson every morning we stayed overnight at her house. The Daily Lesson is based on a theme which changes each week (God is Truth, for instance), with passages from the Bible coordinated with passages from *Science and Health with Key to the Scriptures* by "our revered leader" Mary Baker Eddy. I can still remember the feel of the thin crinkly pages and the slight grit of the blue chalk on my fingertips, chalk she used to bracket each passage for the week, which was later easily erased. Because of that chalk I am left with the impression that every revelation is blue.

I grew up among oak trees and salt-grass hills in northern California. Until last month we owned nine-hundred-and-some acres in the valley, what was left of a 10,000-acre Spanish landgrant acquired by my great great great grandfather, Cutler Blight, slowly decimated by drought and my father's drinking.

My father was a farmer—sugar beets, sweet corn, alfalfa—who hated it, wishing instead to be a filmmaker, an artist in the manner of Terrence Malick, which desire his father ridiculed, preferring I guess that he carry on the tradition of homicide. This is him at twenty-three with his hair slicked back and the same sweet face of The Fugitive.

He was strictly a maintenance drinker and never became violent. The only time he raised his voice was when he couldn't find his comb, a long black fine-tooth comb he left on the yellow tile beside the sink in the bathroom. I remember it smelled of hair oil. When this comb was missing (because one of us kids had used it and not put it back), he would begin to curse, and his cursing would fill the house. "God damn son of a bitch can't a man even find a som-bitching comb where he leaves it without having to look all over the Jesus Christ house is that too frigging much to ask in life a God damn son of a bitch comb?" It was so startling to hear this string of cuss words coming from our mild father that we never got used to it. Every time he began (on the order of once or twice a year) it would make us laugh. Pretty soon he would be laughing too, his voice rising higher and higher, like a shrieking girl's, and then it would begin: we would beg him to do his chicken laugh. I don't know why it was called that—I've never heard a chicken laugh—but we all knew what it meant. It was a hysterical sound that began way up high and then lost control, sliding down slowly, chromatically, like an unplugged coyote. No, the closest thing I've heard to it actually is the scream at the beginning of "Wipeout," an instrumental the Safaris did back in the Sixties. When we heard his chicken laugh we would fall on the floor in ordinary laughter, holding our sides, tears running down our faces, happy to be in this crazy family. Even now when I hear anyone say, "God damn son of a bitch," I start to laugh, which as you can imagine is not always appropriate.

I think our father loved us, but his love, unlike his cussing and his laughter, was without passion. He cried more when Patsy Cline died in an airplane crash than he did for his own mother. From that I should have learned that affinity is thicker than blood.

This is my mother at seventeen. Her hair is auburn and, depending on the color she wears, her eyes are blue or green. Her waist was so small that my father could reach around it with two hands, his thumbs and middle fingers touching. She had the kind of beauty that men lie for: say they are professional athletes or millionaires, promise things they will regret in the morning. She married my father, I believe, for the novelty of his indifference.

As a mother she was moody, unpredictable, given to long silences alternating with recriminations, typically beginning with "You always . . ." or "You never . . . ," what followed "always" being of course bad, and what followed "never" good.

What she wanted to be other than a wife and mother, I don't know. Maybe dead. A self-taught pessimist, she read Berryman and Roethke to us at bedtime instead of fairy tales. "Listen to *this*," she'd say, eyes bright, when we were coming to a line she particularly relished, some piercing insight about death or nothingness. From her I learned how, on a low-medium day, to avert my eyes from the positive and throw myself down a well of self-pity. She called this "seeing things clearly." But we could always count on her being there when we got home from school: she was an agoraphobic, a condition only lately named. We called her a homebody. I loved her for her sorrowful face and for the way she brushed my long red hair each night—it was fine and tangled easily—with great consideration, gently, as if mesmerized. I think it soothed her. Standing behind me in my dressing-table mirror, she would say I was a swan, and that one day I would wake up beautiful, thereby laying in me the habit of waiting and dreams of radical transformation.

My mother's own parents—Grandma and Granddad Grimes—were killed in an automobile accident when she was three, and for that reason she was treated as permanently grieving, though I don't believe she remembered them very clearly, except for the picture that stood in place of memory. That woman with the squirrel-faced fur around her neck, posing in front of the black Packard, one foot on the running board, is her mother. Her father is the gentleman with the felt-gray Stetson and one gold front tooth, standing next to her. For a moment I study their expressions to see what they knew, but my grandmother's expression is perfectly blank and my grandfather's face is in shadow, though the brown marble eyes of the fur might be taken as a prediction of grief.

This is my brother Morgan, whose name means "born by the sea," which he wasn't, but which was where my mother wanted to be, instead of on a dusty farm in a hot valley. Here he is looking like a six-foot-three James Dean, same bad attitude. To give just one indication, he killed my twenty-six cats with his .22 the summer I was ten. They weren't house cats of course but ran free in the barn, and I loved them more than any living things, having christened each of them with an appropriate name during a moving ceremony at the edge of the creek: Furry, Midnight, Calico, Whitepaw, and so on (names, I regret to say, not showing much imagination). He knocked them off one a day for twenty-six days because I had done something to displease him.

When he wasn't terrorizing me he'd give me lectures on public relations—how if I'd quit telling the truth at every opportunity, I might be able to wind our mother around my little finger the way he did, with flattery and false promises. But the one thing I do give him credit for is that he introduced me to my future husband.

This is a snapshot of Rich and me with our hands in each other's pockets, the first year we were married and I was pregnant with Sunny. The marriage didn't last but the love did.

Sunny's real name is Raymond, after my father. We called him Sunny because he was so morose. That's him, age two, scowling into the eye of the camera. The first time we took him to the zoo he cried at all the animals in cages. As a baby he could cry longer and louder than the majority of the clinically depressed. It was a wail with a particular pitch that contained both heartbreak and outrage. It was not a sound you could be sympathetic toward every day. I took to wearing earplugs. But then of course I couldn't hear anything else. It was a dilemma.

Sunny stopped crying when he learned to talk. His first word was a sentence. He was sitting in his high chair and I was trying to feed him puréed peas. He shook his head and said, "I can't like it," clearly articulating the *t*s.

Even after he could talk Sunny got on my nerves. Telling the same joke over and over. When he was six: "Bobby, Bobby, did you push your little sister downstairs?" A pause. "No, Ma. I only pushed her down the first step. She fell the rest of the way herself." Maniacal laughter. When he was sixteen: "Why did the chicken cross the road?" To get to the other side? "No, Ma. It was stapled to the punk rocker." In addition to being morose, Sunny has a very sick sense of humor.

At seventeen, after reading *The Sun Also Rises,* Sunny decided to become a writer, and he took to saying, "Wouldn't it be pretty to think so" after every remark I made. That year I gave him a cloth-bound notebook to write his favorite quotations in. He titled it *Sunny's Notebook.* I can still remember the first few entries:

All you have to do is write one true sentence. Write the truest sentence that you know.   Ernest Hemingway

Everything hurts.   Michaelangelo Antonioni
I would rather go mad than enjoy myself.   Antisthenes

But there was none he liked better than "The world is ugly, and the
people are sad." When he first discovered it (from one of my mother's
"bedtime stories"), he'd say it with a straight face in a solemn, mono-
tonic voice, and then laugh until he couldn't breathe. Sunny is someone I love.

After Rich and I got divorced, Sunny and I went home to live on
the ranch in what used to be Uncle Ad's house, a three-story white
clapboard on the other side of the woods. No longer having a real
job to distract me, I began my career in photography. My first por-
traits were of members of my family. Daddy on the harvester, his
face streaked with dust. My mother in a white silk robe, putting on
makeup. Angela holding her breath, her cheeks puffed out like Dizzie
Gillespie's.

My sister Angela is a year and one week older than I am and three
years younger than our brother Morgan. Here she is in a baby blue
cashmere, her long blond hair as flawless as a Breck girl ad. We shared
a room until we were grown: her side pathologically neat, mine
strewn with dirty clothes, rotting pizza, lost homework. As a child her
goal in life was to be perfect and she came very close. She never
fought the way my brother and I did, and she never talked back to our
mother. (I often made a *tsk*-ing sound, conveying a combination of
sarcasm and disgust, which I thought safer than outright revolution
but which would sometimes get my face slapped.) The only fault I can
remember was the way she'd hold her breath until turning blue when
the world didn't go the way she thought it should. My mother and father would start fighting and Angela would puff out her cheeks until
they stopped or she passed out, whichever came first. We called her

The Fixer. Later on her disappointment with reality grew to include political events as well as family disasters. She held a candlelight vigil attended by thirteen virgins dressed in white when President Kennedy was shot, and they played the music from Camelot. She went on a hunger strike when Morgan was drafted and sent to Vietnam. My mother made her quit the day she weighed ninety-four pounds and her green dress hung from her shoulders like a sack. When Martin Luther King was killed, we got the "I have a dream" speech every night at dinner for a month.

Except for this gift for noble gestures that changed nothing, and an unwavering belief in several cracked theories (she "knew," for example, that whenever somebody lost weight, somebody else gained it), she was conventional. In high school she was head majorette, homecoming queen, beautiful, smart, universally admired, a hard act to follow for a skinny bow-legged red-haired girl with a nose that looks like it's been broken at the bridge. But she loved me unconditionally and so I tried to forgive her for being perfect. She often expressed the wish that she could be like me (hell on wheels and who cares), which went a long way toward making me feel at home in the world.

This is me, age seven, lying alone in a field of mustard flower, staring up at the sun, wondering whether it was true, as my mother said, that staring at the sun could cause blindness. I prayed to go blind or to suffer some other tragic loss, so that I could be brave and enigmatic and full of woe and would thereby earn my mother's bereaved smile. There is an aristocracy of great suffering done with grace and I wanted to belong to it.

"Be careful what you pray for," Grandmother Blight used to say when we had finished reading The Daily Lesson.

I lost my right eye in a pool-playing accident at the Sea Horse
Saloon on January first, my thirty-ninth birthday. I'd tell you the story
but everyone I've told it to so far—man or woman—starts making
retching noises and backing away. But you can use your imagination:
a pool cue, a jealous woman, one blue eye.

I was in the hospital for six weeks. You can have too much time
to think. I stared at the white walls so long I went snow-blind. I kept
putting my hand over the bandages on the right side of my face, the
way you do when you're trying to see something more clearly.

When I had been out of the hospital less than a week, my mother
called to say that my brother had been arrested and charged with a vicious crime—killing his ex-wife Arlene—whereupon every member
of our family took sides. Except me. I didn't know which side to take.
So I stood in the middle, wavering.

I went to my ex-husband for diversion and comfort and, com-
pletely without my foreknowledge or consent, a ten-year-old betrayal
was brought to light, thereby altering the past. And not for the better,
I might add.

My father believed my brother did what he was charged with, and
my mother looked up from her big-screen TV long enough to say she
wouldn't sleep with a traitor, so my father moved out of the house
into the Golddust Inn in town and took up full-time drinking at the
Sea Horse, his camcorder sitting beside him on the bar, recording the
dark.

Early that fall my grandmother died in a hospital, the one fate
she'd hoped to avoid, and by Thanksgiving the land was sold to some
Asian businessmen, nearly a thousand acres where we had lived as a
family for six generations—seven counting Sunny—since 1850, the
year California became a state.

When Angela said once again that everything happens for the best, I smacked her.

Then—frosting on the poison cake—I was diagnosed a manic depressive, prescribed lithium and Prozac—in short, cured of my melancholia. And therein lay my grief. I had wanted all my life to get to the black heart of things. I discovered there was no black heart of things, only chaos.

"You're talking too fast," my mother would say. "Nobody can understand a precious word you're saying. Now take a deep breath, and begin again, more slowly."

part one

BITTER LOVE

LOOK AT THIS ONE: BLACK HAIR,
blue eyes, a day's growth of beard. This is where the story begins.

His name was Jake and he was a steam-pipe fitter. He drove a
rusted-out puke-green Maverick that he bought with some money he
won playing liars' dice. There was a hole the size of a bowling ball in
the floorboard. No rugs except for some little frayed pieces of green
still stuck to the metal. The tape player ate every tape you put into it.
I remember how I cried the day it ate my Bonnie Raitt. When you
turned the heater on it smelled like dirty socks burning, and it didn't
put out any heat.

His driving was worse than his car. Every time we went anywhere
together, I'd end up with a knot as big as a fist in my stomach and
violent inner trembling from the many times I'd nearly died. An
eighteen-wheeler would screech to a halt inches from my door, and
he'd smile like a manic child. He looked behind him *after* he changed
lanes, used his rearview mirror mostly for picking his teeth, which
he'd do with a silver dental instrument while driving eighty miles an
hour. When the light, any light, turned green, he'd floor it, apparently
untouched by the months of gas rationing most of us remember. He
took every corner like he was at Indy, cut people off without even a
gesture toward his blinkers, turned on his lights at night only as an

afterthought. He was dangerous.

Two weeks after he left me he wrote me a letter. He said he felt like he'd been driving for a long time through the dark toward some glorious city. That he'd taken the back roads because he couldn't find the main highway. It was a longer route, he knew, but he thought he'd get there eventually. Sometimes he thought he could see lights, but like a mirage of water they would vanish as he got closer. But he kept on driving, too stubborn and stupid to stop and ask someone. What they would have told him, he said, is that that road didn't go there.

I guess I was supposed to be the glorious city. Or maybe it was "true love" he was driving at. I'm not sure. I wanted to write back and say that maybe, it's just a thought, per*haps* he should consider this: the reason he didn't make it to the glorious city is that his car is shit and he's a lousy driver. I wanted to say that there are some good places you can't find on a map. I didn't, of course. I wouldn't want him to think I was bitter.

But he cured me of country music, I'll give him that. I used to drink Jose Cuervo and play Patsy Cline or Hank Williams and cry myself sick. He taught me the true meaning of self-pity. I no longer need the cheap fix.

I remember Patsy was singing the night we met. I had gone to the Sea Horse Saloon in a mood of drink-yourself-blind. I was upset, not about anything in particular but just about the general strain of living—that a person has to *work* for a living, for example. I am a photographer, as I may have said, but because I liked to eat, I was working for Ted's Typing Service at the time, on Pacific Avenue. Drunks off the street would bring you in some legal form to type up—they were suing their landlord, they were writing up their Last Will and Testament—and they would breathe whiskey in your face and threaten you with nonpayment for fixing their spelling errors.

Working at some low-level job for peon wages at great aggravation instead of pursuing one's art, what kind of life is that?

He came in and sat down with two barstools between us. Friendly but not pushy. I looked up out of polite curiosity but just quickly, no smile. Dark hair, a beard, well-built. Pretty blue eyes, so kind, they reminded me of my grandmother's. Some guys, you look into their eyes and know it's only a matter of time until they pick you up and throw you against a wall. This guy wouldn't do it. Or if he did, he'd regret it instantly and forever.

When he smiled I wanted him. It was the kind of smile that would not only take you home and tuck you in afterwards but would fix you breakfast.

"I want! I want!" This is something I would yell at odd moments during our days together. Then Jake would come to me, take off my clothes, first the blouse, unbuttoned slowly from the bottom, each article of clothing—taking his time with me, making me wait, teasing me with his hands, his tongue. "What do you want?" he would say and smile at me like I was really something. Something precious. Something you would always want in your line of sight.

I guess not.

I've been going through some letters he wrote me. Reading them over for clues. He said in one that what he felt for me was not love because love was not fierce enough. But reading that didn't make me feel better. If someone has decided to rewrite the past, old letters prove nothing.

Maybe he didn't like having someone around who was always pointing out the half-eaten worm in the rotten apple. I have a gift for the negative, I admit. But even those who are difficult need to be loved, and in that I am no exception.

He had a complicated system of merits and demerits as to love.

How harsh you were last night to my friend, Alex. That's seven demerits. Janice and Rick *liked* you, that's three for you. Why must you keep badmouthing Big John? Don't you know that'll cost you an arm and a leg? It was hard that last year when he was doing the final tally. Sometimes I would see him moving his lips and know that he was adding things up, trying to be fair. It would be interesting to know which point was the clincher. Big John, maybe.

Big John was Jake's boss. He didn't appreciate me. He had his yes-men around him and he didn't want anyone disturbing the consensus: great man, great pipe fitter. He even wrote a book about it and those boys read it as if it were the Bible. They could quote it chapter and verse.

I think Jake thought of Big John as his father. His real father walked out on him and his mother when he was in kindergarten, after brutalizing him a little so he would remember dear old Dad. Maybe that's where he got the talent.

He was always walking out. This is the picture that sticks in my mind: him slamming his things together and stuffing them into the trunk of his Maverick. It would take several trips, and he would keep his face in a rage the whole time. He walked this ridiculous indignant cartoon strut when he was mad. I'd be crying, wondering what went wrong this time, saying I was sorry, or saying I wished I'd never put myself in his hands, whichever was appropriate.

He hated what he called "scenes." That's me screaming and him stuffing his things into the trunk of his Maverick. But he wouldn't talk to you in an ordinary human voice about anything of significance. I would try to get him drunk, hoping he would tell me where I stood, once and for all. But he could never tell me the truth, as if it took some superhuman courage he just couldn't summon. So I was always trying to read the signs, begging for bad news. "It looks like you don't love me enough," I would say softly. "But maybe you don't have the guts to tell me." We'd be at the Sea Horse, listening to "You're Not the Man" on the jukebox, that saxophone like someone moaning. "No," he'd say, too carefully. "I love you." But the look of his eyes in the light of the Coors sign was not convincing. Finally it was me who'd get drunk and start screaming. Patience is not its own reward.

If I knew his side of the story, I would tell it. But here I am as usual having to make it up, trying to stuff all these painful memories and ragged feelings into some kind of trunk. I hate people—I'm trying for a light tone here—who have no sense of an ending, no need of a proper burial.

When I got that temporary job down in L.A. (photographing zoo animals) and he moved in to the latest new place that was chosen without me in mind, he got rid of my favorite chair. Looking back, that was a sign.

He took up with this woman, Sally. Dumb as shit and bright pink lipstick. That was the second sign. I guess she was a glorious city he could find on his frayed atlas. Her idea of independence was to always have more than one lover. I used to ridicule this.

Some people, when they are gone, leave you less than you were. He wasn't one of these. There were good things.

For example, presents. He was always giving me presents—books he thought I would like, little knick-knacks—once a candle snuffer, once a small carved wooden box he'd made himself—sometimes flowers, home-made greeting cards with confetti in them for my birthday. This time it was a white candle in a brass candle holder with a little ring at the base you can hold with your finger. At first I thought it was not one of his best efforts. But then he took my hand and led me into the bathroom. It was all cleaned up, clean towels, the floor scrubbed, a plant on the shelf behind the old porcelain tub, a fluffy new rug on the floor. He had the bathtub filled almost to the edge, just the temperature I like it: hot enough to burn your skin. He set the candle on the tile in front of the mirror and lit it. Vanilla. He put a rolled towel at the bottom of the door to get rid of the last natural light. Then he helped me take off my clothes, tie up my hair. He told me to blow out the candle and put the towel back at the bottom of the door when he went out, then he left. For once I did what he said. Then I lay in the scalding water up to my neck for almost an hour, until the water was cold, my skin was withered, and my brain was quiet. Nothing ever soothed me so much except drugs. After that when I would be anxious and full of grief he'd say, "How about a dark bath?"

And he was funny. He had this schtick he liked to do. Somebody would be twisting and turning for attention, wearing too much makeup, say, or with a dress cut down to her belly button—anyway, trying too hard—and he'd put his left wrist at the crown of his head, use the fingers for bangs, put his other index finger in his chin dimple and say, in this lisping Shirley Temple voice, "Am I pretty, Mama?" He knew how to amuse me.

We had what he called "weekend adventures." We would do something we'd never done before, maybe something slightly scary. Once we went up in a balloon over San Francisco. I had to drink three straight shots of tequila to get up enough courage, but I did it. Another time we went to the mud baths in Calistoga. Mud doesn't hide much. There is something very sexy about the human body covered with mud. That night in Calistoga was a good night.

It was in the spirit of our weekend adventures that I bought him this white silk teddy for his birthday. Me in it was the present. But I was too shy to put it on. He kept asking and I finally did. He had me turn this way and that in the soft light in the dark room. He looked at me then like he loved me enough. I can remember every instant of that night, the urgency, my pounding heart, the way I moved above him. Those are the memories that make the loss of an eye seem a kindness.

I've never had a talent for sleeping. Four or five hours a night is usual. But when he left I woke up crying every night at three a.m. and couldn't get back to sleep. I have, since I was very young, seen movies on my eyelids. It happens when I'm falling asleep. My eyelids are half-closed (neither all the way open nor all the way closed seems to work as well), my eyelashes filtering the dark. I regulate my breathing by humming "Shepherd Show Me How to Go," an old hymn from childhood that Grandmother Blight taught me, and I rock back and forth to quiet my brain. Then it begins: the flash of lights and movement, faces coming into focus, disappearing, words as vivid as if someone had just spoken.

Angela has a theory about why this happens. Our dad had us watching his home-made movies before we could think. Sometimes he would wake us up in the middle of the night to view a scene he was particularly proud of, a scene in which he thought he had made the edit just right, or a good transition. So somewhere deep in the hard-wiring of our brains, Angela says, are flickering images and unhappy endings, all mixed up with the love of our father.

After Jake left it began to happen against my will. Images of us together, in different postures, filled my head. Every night, like a video, I would see us.

Pale thighs against a dark-haired chest. I am sitting on his lap, in the large red leather chair, my knees up under his armpits. I am rocking back and forth, back and forth. He is making a sound I have never heard before, his eyes half-closed, his mouth open. I kiss him hard, bite his bottom lip until I taste blood.

After a month I went to see Dr. Glass, whose name I found in the Yellow Pages. I said, "I can't sleep." There were blue shadows under my eyes. I said, "If you're not careful you can see through my skin." I held up my translucent wrists, helpless. "I see him. I see him everywhere." She said it was only grief.

Then she recommended something called counterimagining. "For example." She held up her two forefingers like goal-posts. "Imagine putting all his letters in a box in the back yard. Burn it. Or," she said, "put *him* in a closet. Now firmly close the door."

I liked this idea. But it didn't work. I cried at the pyre of letters, let him out after five minutes.

But she'd given me a thought. That's when I started trying to imagine a better ending, thinking this might allow me to put this man behind me, give me some peace.

This is the way it really happened. He called me to say it was over. Just like that. I had been supposed to come and stay with him that weekend, to celebrate my birthday and New Year's Eve. I thought we had been working things out. I had been trying to change in some of the ways he needed (for example, quit screaming), trying to fathom what it was like to be him, trying to understand what made him the man he was. Now I know: too much sympathy can kill you.

Anyway, he calls up and after five minutes of clearing his throat like he was choking on a God damn chicken bone—and slow me saying, "What? What is it? Can't you *breathe?*"—he just says this: "I don't want us to be together anymore. I don't want you to come up here this weekend."

I asked him why. He said he didn't think he could make it clear. I said, "Try." He said that living with me was like riding on a roller coaster and he wanted to get off. He said he loved me but not enough. He said there was someone else.

"That's pretty clear," I said. "Jesus Christ, any one of those reasons would have been sufficient."

But he said he was trying to be honest for once. Nice change for him, I thought, but I was trying to keep from being beaten to death by my own heart. And I'd bought a nonrefundable ticket.

Telling me over the phone like that—I didn't think it showed respect for what we had been to each other. We'd had a life together (four years, on and off) and I deserved better than a phone call. I was almost thirty-nine but I'd already learned that it's not so much what is done to you as the manner in which it is done.

So I used the ticket. Air West. Free drinks. During takeoff I closed my eyes and the images started to come. Now it wasn't just at night, when I couldn't sleep. Thoughts of him were taking over my life. I closed my eyes tighter but the images still came.

This time we're standing on the balcony overlooking the ocean. It is night. I have my long black nightgown on, the one with spaghetti straps. I stand in front, the top railing just above my waist, an edge against my ribs. He is behind, the only warmth in the cold night, his thighs against the backs of my thighs. He slips the spaghetti straps off my shoulders, cups his warm hands under my breasts, uses his thumb and forefinger to make me arch my back. I can hear someone on the beach, calling, and I can see the light of an oil tanker in the distance. The salt air stings my nostrils, and though the water is too far away I believe I can feel the sea spray against my skin. I feel him lift the slippery material up to my waist, feel him push himself inside me, easy at first, then harder. By now I'm holding on to the railing at the last joint of my fingers, afraid I'll go over, head first, into the sand. But I don't think this is the appropriate time to bring it up. I'm also worried that the people next door might be watching, since I don't hear their TV set turned on. Then he says my name against my hair, "Sarah," and I forget all about it—the risk of falling, the voyeurs next door, every-thing. I stand on tiptoe, feel my feet rise off the wooden planks as I watch the white of the slow-breaking waves.

Liar! I started tying him up, first his arms, behind his back, hand-cuffed to emphasize a point, then his legs. When I was through he couldn't move. I made the rope so tight it burned his ankles. *Betrayer!* I put masking tape over his mouth. He made a "Mm-mmm" sound, but this time I didn't give in. A person has limits.

When the flight attendant came to take my plastic glass I looked down and it was crushed in my hand, just like in a beer commercial.

I got into town around eight that evening and took a cab to the Sea Horse, knowing he would be there with his latest glorious city. I thought I deserved a more fitting ending and I intended to have it.

The cab driver was tight-lipped and sullen (New Year's Eve and he had to work) but I gave him a twenty-dollar tip, for flair and courage, then walked through the heavy black curtains. Made an en-trance, you might say.

This woman, call her Poughkeepsie, was bigger than I expected. Hair the color of mouse. Thin. Pale. Not too glamorous. No Paris.

I remember the song on the jukebox. Lenny Welch. "Since I Fell For You." Jesus.

I walked up to the bar where they were sitting with their backs to me. I said, "Hi, my name's Sarah," and stuck out my hand. I can be civilized when I have to be. But she didn't seem to understand my de-sire to have things out with the man whose thigh she had her hand on, just looked at me with her cool appraising eyes, perfect eyeliner. So I tried to give her a little history, let her know where I stood in the order of things.

"Fuck off," she explained.

I grabbed the dice cup and shook the bartender, Doris, for the music. I lost. But she gave me four quarters anyway. I put on Hank Williams singing "Your Cheatin' Heart" with "I'm So Lonesome I Could Cry" as a chaser. Six times.

I had a few more Tequila Sunrises and then tried to convince her again. "Four years," I said. "You are only a few nights. Maybe *good* nights, but still . . ."

She was not impressed with this line of reasoning and pushed me backwards off the barstool where I had been trying to make my case.

Then she said, out of meanness or spite, "Me and Jake—we spent last weekend fucking our brains out."

I said, from a back-floating position, "I bet it didn't take all weekend."

All this time Jake is looking at me like I'm in the wrong movie. I thought, *Jake. It's me. Sarah. Don't you recognize me?* At my final undoing, I had believed, at my attempted massacre, he would be on my side. No. Maybe she was a few more nights than I imagined.

I was down and I didn't have the will to get up. I just laid there, near defeat, close to a whimper. The boots around my head seemed way too big for human feet.

That's when Big John, Jake's boss, walked in. He looked at Jake, then down at me. He said, "I see you've finally found your place in life."

This gave me a little incentive. But when I picked myself up off the floor Poughkeepsie was right in my face. That's when I picked up the pool cue. Never pick up a pool cue if you don't intend to use it. Never brandish a pool cue at someone larger and meaner than yourself. I play these useless admonitions over and over in my head, the way a person might repeat a prayer for improved health over the deceased.

I had believed the human eye to be a tenacious thing. I think that woman must have been an oyster shucker before she took up with Jake. She popped that thing out of there as easy as opening a longneck, like removing a cork with a crowbar, like playing tiddly winks. I thought my face was on fire. I tried to put it out with my fingernails.

My last memory is of Jake saying, "I'm sorry, Sarah, I'm sorry, Sarah, I'm so sorry, Sarah," as if by incantation and regret the lost eye might be called back.

I was in the hospital for six weeks. I thought about Jake, the old movies, the old reruns. No counterimagining could touch the way his skin felt next to my skin, like you're in warm water and sinking.

This time we're in bed on Christmas Eve. He has given me a toy and we are trying it out, children laughing in the dark. "Like this?" he says, moving the head of the machine. "Like this?" I wiggle until it's where I want it, then I begin to writhe, making sounds of mock ecstasy. He takes me almost roughly, his thrusting hard and steady, his hands on my shoulders, holding them down, as if he were trying to teach me a lesson, his thrusting now hard and irregular, probing, as if he were trying to locate the wound. I don't know him. My eyes are wide open and the only sound in the room is the muffled whirring of the small motor trapped in the blue comforter.

When the candy striper lady brought in Jake's letter I regarded it calmly, approaching indifference. I thanked her and set it on the nightstand and didn't look at it for three minutes at least. In my secret heart I expected it to restore the past. It would say, "I didn't know how much I loved you until you almost died." Words to that effect.

The way it began in reality was this:

Dear Sarah,
As you know, I've never been very committed to this relationship.

That was followed by the driving-in-the-dark-toward-the-glorious-city bullshit. When I got to the part that said, "We started out as friends. That won't change, I hope," I tore the letter up into little pieces and ate it, I was that angry.

My last week in the hospital the candy striper lady brought in some books on a cart, but she didn't smile. She looked at me as if hers were a serious mission, full of mortality and risk. I picked out *Crooked Hearts*. I looked up at her. She shook her head back and forth, eyes that saw everything. I put the book back on the cart.

She handed me instead a little book of meditations, which made me think of Sunny, wondering if I'd find something he might like, something to write down in his notebook.

The passage I concentrated on was about *amor fati,* loving one's fate even when it's harsh, especially when it's harsh. Nietzsche. What he's talking about is pain, great pain, that long, slow pain in which we are burned with green wood, pain that takes its time with us, like a good lover.

The morning they took the bandages off and I saw the place where my eye had been, I cried. Tears seeping through the red twisted skin. An obscene wink. It was the most sickening sight I had ever seen, and it was a permanent part of my face. But I refused the black patch. I have made a lot of mistakes in my life but I am not a coward.

Nietzsche says that only this kind of pain forces us to go down into our depths, to put away all trust, all good-naturedness, all that would veil, all mildness, all that is medium—things in which we have formerly found our humanness.

For days I howled like a coyote. I could not look in a mirror. I wanted, more than to be whole again, someone to hold me. But when the candy striper lady came in I tried to be stoical. I said, "Nothing is as good when you have it as it is bad when it's gone." It didn't ring true. I said, "Rejection is the great aphrodisiac." She looked skeptical. "I have been wounded in an accident of my own choosing, and there is no way I can undo it." She fluffed up the pillows and walked out, having given no sign of agreement or dissent. I hung out my hand like a handkerchief—*"Please"*—but she didn't look back.

Out of such long and dangerous exercises in self-mastery, Nietzsche says, one emerges as a different person, with a few *more* question marks—above all, with the will to question more persistently, more deeply, severely, harshly, evilly, and quietly than has ever been questioned on this earth before. The trust in life is gone; life itself has become a problem.

I'm not a religious person, but when I read that part I thought of Grandmother Blight and The Daily Lesson and though there was no one to hear it I said it out loud: "Amen."

"I'm going to teach you a little game called Russian Roulette. Do you want to play?" Morgan asked.

It sounded like a card game, something with a roulette wheel, so I said, "Yes."

We were out in the barn, sitting on the fence that separates the hay-filled middle section of the barn from the two long sides with stanchions, our toes tucked back between the lower slats for balance. He leaned over backward without unwinding his feet and took a pistol from behind a bale of hay, and then he rose up and took a bullet from his pocket.

"Here's how you play," he said, smiling. "Put one bullet in the gun, then spin the chamber. Like this." He pushed the bullet in with his thumb, clicked the cartridge shut. Then he spun it around twice with the flat of his hand, like playing a cymbal. He put it to my head.

I could feel the metal against my temple, the keyhole of the barrel and the gunsight. My heart started beating hard and I felt my temple throbbing against the metal, felt the metal digging in. I was scared to move.

"Are you ready?" he asked.

"No. I don't want to play." I looked down and the muscle in my thigh had begun to twitch. It jumped like a small animal and even my hand on it did not make it stop.

He laughed his crazy laugh. "I *asked* you if you wanted to play, didn't I? I gave you a free choice, and I dis-*tinct*-ly heard you say *yes.*"

I didn't know what to reply to this. It was true, but distorted. If somebody asked you if you wanted to play a game, were you wrong to expect something good, wrong to feel duped if the game ended with him blowing your brains out?

I felt him cock the gun, felt it dig into my scalp as he pulled back the hammer. "Think of it as a little test," he said, "to see if the world values your presence." Then he laughed again, his Boris Karloff laugh but with more malice in it.

By this time my whole body was trembling, and I was afraid my shaking would make the gun go off accidentally, and I tried very hard to hold still but could not stop shaking.

"Ready?" he said again. "On the count of three. *One. Two.*" He waited and I noticed I'd quit breathing, all I could feel was my heart moving in my chest and my head, both places at once.

"Three."

Click.

I cried out, put my hand to my temple, then looked at it. No blood, only sweat.

"So far, so good," he said, spinning the cartridge again.

That's when I started to cry in earnest.

"Oh poor baby," he said in a voice like Elmer Fudd's. "Her doesn't wike the widdle game? Her doesn't want to *pway* anymore?"

"Please," I said, "please."

"Does the prisoner have a last request?"

My mind leaped and darted like a bat in a closet, flying into walls, falling through darkness. I could run, but then he'd shoot me. I could grab the gun, but he was bigger and would take it back. I could knock him over and get out of the barn before he knew what hit him, but he could run faster than I could and would catch me. I could . . . Every way was grief.

Then I quit adding it up, the possible rewards of every action, the likely cost, what he would do if I did this, what I would do next, and if he didn't—it all stopped. And at that second I believed I was free, there was only what I *would* do, and he could no longer touch me.

I unwound my legs from the fence, climbed carefully down, and walked out of the barn.

He yelled out "Stop!" but I didn't stop. I kept walking and I felt powerful.

When I got outside I slammed the barn doors closed and ran back to the house, crying hysterically, screaming and laughing. I fell down once on the gravel road and my knee was skinned and bleeding but I didn't feel it. There was no one home, no one to save me. I hid in my father's closet. I sat in the dark on the floor of the closet and smelled the familiar smell of him. I felt my arms and legs trembling, and I pulled down one of his flannel shirts to comfort me. I stayed there in the dark of the closet, petting my father's shirt, until I heard a car in the driveway, and knew someone was home.

I never told my parents what he'd done. I never told anyone. I'm not sure why but my best explanation is this: They couldn't stop him anyway, and then he'd know I'd told. And a person who is crazy and angry is more dangerous than a person who is crazy.

This is the photograph that stands for that day. I am eight, red hair in French braids, yellow ribbons; Morgan is twelve, already six feet tall, a too-short flat top giving his face an odd shape—he with his "barrel" finger at the temple of my head, his thumb cocked, the middle finger ready, a smile twisting his face. My hand is wrapped around his finger, trying to break it. It is a pose characteristic of that time, to remind me of what he could do if he chose. "Everyone sleeps," he said.

⊙

BEFORE THE ACCIDENT I HAD USED my right eye for my work, squinting with my left, moving through the world with authority and speed, seeing exactly what I wanted to capture, taking it. Photography was the only area of my life in which I knew who I was, in which I had confidence.

If you look very closely you can see the phantom eye weeping. I am the ruined instrument. I am the cracked compass, its needle whirling madly, charting the course to the real world. I am the lightbeam that, finding its own eye, believes its tears to be an undiscovered ocean.

This is the first black-and-white I took after my encounter with the pool cue, made tentatively, using a tripod and self-timer because I could no longer see with my right eye. It may sound like a trivial thing, but the result was that I could not count on instincts that had taken a lifetime to develop. If you think it would be easy, try cutting off your right hand and writing with your left. Imagine a concert pianist after shock treatments, his memory gone, his fingers clumsy stubs, his reasonable grief. Lovemaking after a mastectomy.

From that day on I had to imagine the pictures I was taking, since I could not look through the lens and so never saw what the film recorded until the print was made. In a way I let the camera see for me.

I spent the morning I got out of the hospital in my darkroom, redoing this print until it looked just like I wanted: perverse, stark, frightening. That accomplished, I went to bed. But I couldn't sleep, couldn't even relax. I looked out my back window, past the baled hay covered with a black tarp, past the pond, toward my parents' house to see if there was a light in the laundry room window. But even my good eye blurred. If you want to know the truth, I was terrified. My mind darted and darted, trying to find a way around the hideous wound, trying to imagine myself well and whole. I kept thinking how satisfying life was when I'd only been deserted and not yet permanently deformed. The way you feel when you get a paper cut that hurts and hurts and won't give you any peace, and you have a vivid sense of what your life was like just preceding it. Easy. Good.

The telephone rang and I got up to answer it but I stopped half-way there, frozen in midgesture as in a game of statues. I knew it wasn't Jake, and if it wasn't Jake it was someone else, someone I didn't want to talk to, except if it was Sunny, which was unlikely since he was in France and had no money, or Angela, and if it was Angela, she could call me back. It was the first time in my life I hadn't answered the telephone when it rang and I felt mildly amazed. One of my ratlike habits was broken and there was the brief hope that I would emerge as some-one else, someone with a different face.

I got back in bed but I couldn't sleep. My eyes felt like somebody had taken steel wool to them. Correction: *eye*. I wanted for someone to take care of me. Jake. I wanted Jake. I wanted to call him. I knew I shouldn't. I knew it was a case of love your torturer because at least he's paying attention, but when could knowledge ever compete with love? Don't be a fool. He left you. Walked out. And then he stood there watching while slut-of-the-month put your eye out. But the hands. Remember the hands?

After fifteen minutes or so of such reflections I dialed the number. It rang five times. His answering machine was turned on, probably permanently, because he couldn't take a chance on me calling him and him having to answer. What would he say? Bruce Springsteen played in the background. "Tunnel of Love." Then a voice, even, controlled, seductive as a sex therapist's voice: "I'm sorry I can't come to the phone right now, but if you'll leave a message after the tone, I'll get back to you as soon as I can."

He's sorry he can't come to the phone and I've lost an eye. I waited for the beep. "My eye," I said and then could think of nothing else so I hung up.

It was by now 4:30, the time of day when if you're not suicidal yet you soon will be. The light is dying. All the children are tired and whining in the streets. The only thing on TV is *Geraldo*. Maybe everything is a fraud.

I dialed Angela's number. She picked it up on the first ring.

"What were you doing, sitting on top of the phone?"

She laughed. "No, I was just passing by on my way to the refrigerator for more Ben and Jerry's Chocolate Fudge Brownie ice cream." For spiritual solace Angela eats. Last month, she insists, she gained the three and a half pounds some other woman lost. She would like to know who to blame.

"I want to call Jake."

"Don't."

"Okay, I called him. But he wasn't there. I left a message. One that showed great restraint."

"What did you say?"

"*My eye*. That's all. *My eye*. Why did I say that? I don't know why I said that." I started to cry.

She said, "Jake's dead," which had become her refrain since the accident. "Next time call me. Anytime you want to call the heartless S.O.B. , call me instead. How is your eye?"

"There's a dull throb behind the one that's missing. I guess 'behind' is the wrong way to put it. There's a dull throb where my right eye once was. But it's not so bad. Sometimes I forget it even happened. Until I wake up. Until I go to the bathroom to brush my teeth. It makes me think of that Leonard Cohen song: 'There's a funeral in the mirror and it's stopping at your face.'"

"Oh Sarah." Her voice has my grief in it.

"How am I going to live with this?"

"I don't know. I'll think of something. In the meantime just don't call Jake," she said.

"I won't. I promise."

After I hung up I tried to take my mind off myself, to amuse myself with various things. I turned on the TV, started clicking from one channel to the next, flinching at each scene—a knife in someone's chest, a gang of men on horses shooting at a lone rider, a building blowing up, people jumping from burning windows, a woman being choked: her scarf caught in the closed subway doors, the train starting to leave, a man holding on. I thought of Angela and as a form of political protest I clicked it off. For a while I flipped through old *Photography* magazines that were piled on the coffee table, letting them slither to the floor. Then I studied the singles ads in the *Manteca Bulletin*, imagining the one I could write now, guaranteed to get attention and no response.

One-eyed woman, 39, would like to meet . . .

I called Jake's number again. Five rings. The same old recording, same seductive voice. While the phone was ringing I thought of the morning the alarm clock went off while we were making love, and neither of us wanted to interrupt what we were doing long enough to shut it off. I remembered the ringing and the light coming through the Venetian blinds, making a pattern of shadows on the bed, and his hands moving through those shadows.

"Jake," was all I said before hanging up.

The next day I didn't get out of bed, except to rewind *Anna* on the VCR, which I had moved along with the TV into my bedroom. I would stand on one foot, hopping in a circle, reciting "Humpty Dumpty sat on a wall, Humpty Dumpty had a great fall" at the top of my lungs, as the VCR whirred, returning me to the beginning. Then, exhausted, I would lie on the dark blue sheets trying to discern some image in the water splotches on the ceiling, trying to remember poems my mother had read to me as a child. All I could remember were isolated lines. "Life, friends, is boring." "My geranium is dying." And certain fragments. "O body swayed to music, O brightening glance." "Nothing that is not there and the nothing that is."

I got a bottle of Mezcal and a large box of Wheat Thins to keep by my bed. I discovered that you can eat Wheat Thins lying down. If you let them soak on your tongue for a while, you don't even have to chew.

Not unmindful of the importance of order, I established a kind of routine. Go to bed at two in the morning. Wake around three, jerk the sheets and blankets around for several hopeless minutes, cry with self-pity and rage, sleep fitfully until five or so, then waken for good, hate the day, eat a few crackers, drink a little tequila, switch on the VCR, leaving the sound off so the people on the screen looked as stupid as they were in real life, their actions as futile. Pursue a line of thought for a few minutes: Nothing matters and so what if it did? Drop it. Pursue another line of thought: Why live when you can have a nice funeral at no expense to yourself? Imagine Jake in some new city. Then mentally tie him up, avoiding the eyes insofar as possible.

I tried to believe Angela who said, "This too will pass," but such moods come with their own spurious certainty, certainty that there is no light at the end of the tunnel, only the tunnel, and no end to that. The only hope of change is that the tunnel appears to be getting smaller, crawling has become necessary, it's getting hard to breathe.

"It's all for the best," Angela said. "You'll see." In spite of experience, Angela had an unflagging faith in the good order of things. It was the kind of uncritical optimism that I detested—the belief that everyone did the best they could, that whatever happened was for the best, or at the very worst was meant to teach you some valuable lesson. The-baby-was-born-braindead-to-teach-us-pity school of philosophy.

When the brain is deprived of sleep for too many nights it begins to think of death as one way to get a little peace and quiet. I was writing out my Last Will and Testament on a form I had saved from Ted's Typing Service when the phone rang and, buoyed by the thought of self-destruction, I answered it.

"Where've you been? I've been calling for days. Every day, every night, at all different times, I let it ring and ring. I've been out of my mind with worry. If you hadn't answered this time I was ready to send your dad over." The calm voice of my mother.

"I've been in the hospital. Since then I haven't been answering the phone." I didn't point out that she might actually have *come over to see* what had become of me. It was all of a quarter mile away.

"Angela said she talked to you." This was in the spirit of an accusation.

"Well, then, you knew I was still kicking."

"What happened? Are you all right?"

"My eye," I said, and began to cry in open self-pity.

"What, honey? What? Tell me."

"I lost my eye. My *right* eye," I added with emphasis, as if this were worse.

"What do you mean you *lost* it?"

"I mean it's gone. *Pffft.* Where my eye used to be is a hole. Well, not a hole really, a twisted absence."

"Honey, I'm so sorry. How did it happen?"

"Jake."

"Ahhh." She'd met Jake. She'd heard the stories. "Do you want me to come over?" This was, for a woman afraid to leave her own house, a generous offer.

"No, Mom. There's nothing for you to do here. I'm going to be fine. Just as soon as I figure out what you can do better with one eye than you can do with two."

"Sarah?" There was a long silence. "I don't know if this is the time to tell you . . ."

I knew she would anyway so I said, "Go ahead."

"Your brother was just arrested. The police came, three black cars with their sirens wailing all the way down the dirt road. Didn't you hear them? It was enough to wake the dead."

I had heard them. But I'd thought the screaming was internal.

"I looked out to see what all the excitement was about and they were handcuffing Morgan with his hands behind his back, just like in the movies."

I hate to admit it, but my first thought was, Of course. Of course this would happen. When a person kills his little sister's twenty-six cats, this is what you can expect.

"What did he do?"

"I don't know. I called up and asked Leona Marie what was going on, but she just kept saying, Oh God, Oh my God, and then she was crying, and Matt and Billy were crying, and I didn't know what to do," she said, starting to cry herself.

"Mom, I lost my eye. Jake left me. I'm depressed enough as it is. I can't listen to this."

"I'm sorry." I believed I could hear her lips tighten, see her eyes refocus in a look of pure meanness. But like my father always said, If you don't like your mother's mood, wait a few seconds. She changes it oftener than her underwear.

"I'll talk to you later in the week," I said.

"Let me know if there's anything I can do. But it's probably better if you don't dwell on it. It's all mud under the bridge."

Wisdom for the ages. "Goodbye, Mom," I said, my face clenched like a fist.

I tried to imagine my six-foot-three brother in some tiny cell, the place he'd put so many people himself when he was a cop. Would he sit there quietly in contained rage, or have his fists wrapped around the bars screaming obscenities? Either way, it was cosmic justice, a little sister's dream, I thought, and was ashamed.

From the third-floor attic
window the ground looked far away. I could see the chickens pecking
the peatdust but they seemed more like mechanical toys than live animals. The sheet was knotted too tightly around my neck and I was
trying to loosen it, pulling at it with my nail-bitten fingers.

"Hold still," Morgan said. "I'm trying to fix the back. If it's all the
same length it will catch the wind."

"There isn't any wind," I said, putting my hand out palm up.

"The air, stupid. Catch the *air.*"

"I'm not going to jump." I backed up a little and he pushed me
forward, then jerked on the tail of the sheet to bring me back. "Hold
still, God damn it!"

"I won't jump."

"Of *course* you will. You *said* you would." His voice was singsong,
full of malice. "You'd be a little sissy *cry*baby if you didn't jump."

I thought about this. I didn't want to be called a sissy or a crybaby.
I didn't think I was a sissy or a crybaby. But I didn't want to jump. Still,
being a sissy or a crybaby might be better than being dead or crippled
for life.

"I won't jump. You can't make me."

"I'll give you ten dollars if you jump."

Ten dollars. With two more dollars I could buy Kerrie Moore's two-wheeler. If I lived. Mine had a flat tire with so many patches in it that it could no longer be fixed, and a rusted out back fender from being left in the creek overnight last Halloween when Morgan scared me as I came over the bridge and I skidded sideways into the muddy water.

"Twelve dollars," he said.

I held out my open hand, to let him know who he was talking to. I wasn't going to jump now and hope to get paid later. I had learned something from experience.

"Do I *look* like a bank?" he said, pulling out two pinches of the front of his T-shirt for inspection.

I yanked at the sheet knotted around my neck, by which I hoped to suggest that until the money was forthcoming I wouldn't be going anywhere fast.

"Okay, I'll go get it." His voice was tired, full of contempt. "Wait right here."

I looked out across the land that stretched as far as I could see. The wheat was high in the midday sun. I shielded my eyes with my hand and saw my dad in the distance on the harvester, cutting a clean track through the gold. I called out to him, knowing he could not hear me. "Daddy." I cupped my hands around my mouth, like someone in a movie, calling. "*Daaaaa-deeeee.*" He looked up, as if he'd heard, but then turned right at the end of a row and his face was lost in the sun.

A slight breeze came up and I thought that if I was going to jump, it would be better to do it now, while there was a wind. I made a pose like Superman, arms straight up, fingers together, as if the right pose might subvert the laws of gravity.

I saw my brother coming across the field from the house. I didn't want to jump anymore, not even for twelve dollars. I wanted to live, with unbroken arms and legs, with my same face. I jerked at the sheet around my neck and it came loose.

He was breathing hard when he got to the top of the attic stairs. There was sweat on his upper lip and it made me afraid. "What the hell do you think you're doing?"

"I changed my mind," I said. "I don't think I want to do any flying today." I put some emphasis on *today* and tried to make my voice casual but I backed against the wall as I spoke.

His eyes went wild. *Crazy eyes,* I thought, whenever he looked like that. *Crazy eyes, get out of the way.* That's how you know someone will do you serious damage, that intensity at the core of the iris, where the soul shows through.

"You said you were going to jump and you're God damn well going to jump, if I have to help you." Spit flew out of his mouth when he talked, which I thought unattractive. His eyes deepened from hazel to green. He studied me for a minute as if he were considering some new possibility he liked the idea of. He smiled, gestured with his hands like a magician before a trick. Then he came up behind me and put his forearm around my neck from the back. He squeezed and I started to choke.

"Which will it be?"

At first I didn't know what he meant. Then he pressed on my windpipe again and it came to me: If I didn't jump he would choke me to death or choke me until I passed out or until somebody stopped him, which was unlikely, since no one knew we were up here in the attic of the old house where Uncle Ad used to live. He jerked his forearm up tight under my chin. I looked out across the field and my eyes teared. I saw the wheat through the blur and I wondered how someone who loved me could let this happen. Mama. Daaaa-deeee. I saw myself as if from above and felt sorry for that child with only herself to save her.

"Let go, you crazy bastard!" I used the back of my head as a weapon and tried to hit his face. I struck something hard, maybe a tooth.

"Little bitch!" He jerked his forearm tighter around my neck. Now my feet dangled above the ground and I was running in midair, the next best thing to a roadrunner cartoon.

"Well?" he said and laughed. "Do you want to fly or shit your pants?"

I jammed my right elbow into his groin. He cried out and I knew my point had hit home. He lost his hold on my neck and the air in my lungs was a sudden pleasure.

He pushed me toward the edge of the window. My feet skittered sideways, a kind of dance, but I righted myself. "I won't go. I will not go willingly. No I said no I won't—"

He pushed me again, a large flat palm against my back, and I was afraid I'd end up face down in the dirt with a broken neck to go with the crooked red S on my home-made cape. I took a deep breath, and I jumped.

This is the picture that gives me back that day, nearly whole.

I went through all the family albums I had, looking for relevant pictures, taking them out, the little black corners that held them snapping from the strain.

I took pictures of the pictures and made eight-by-ten prints, so that something lost in the snapshot might be in this manner revealed. Exaggeration was my method. All that morning I watched the familiar faces bloom in the dark water.

I strung up a clothesline in front of the picture window in the family room and attached the eight-by-ten prints with wooden clothespins. The last print is of my brother holding a marksman's trophy he won when he was a cop, the best shooter in the state of California. It's hanging by one corner because the clothespins ran out, and it gives my brother a forlorn look, as if he were falling slowly in space, the movements so minute that no one watching sees.

THE NEXT MORNING I CALLED
Ted's Typing Service. I needed money for chemicals—to develop my
photographs. I had also become fond of eating and I was down to my
last five hundred dollars. I needed either a job or a new credit card.

Faya answered. Faya is fond of designer drugs. It's her one and
only recreation. Every Monday morning, during the four years I
worked there, she would come into the office and tell everyone
within earshot about her weekend trip. The last one I'd heard about
was called Ecstasy. She said, It was.

"How are you doing?" she asked now. "Long time no see. Been
staying out of trouble?"

"Fine," I said. "I've been just fine. Is Ted there?"

"Just a minute, I'll get him. Don't take any wooden nickels.
By-eee."

"Hello?" He sounded like he expected a crank call.

"Ted, this is Sarah Blight. Remember me? I've been in the hospital since that L.A. job. I'm calling to see if I might get my job back.
Don't forget how fast I am. A hundred and twenty words a minute." I
tried to sound cheerful. Ted likes false cheer.

"Well, Sarah, I don't see why not. We need someone here. In fact,
we just got a three-hundred page manuscript that the guy needs

by next week, *Cosmology for Two*. And you *were* always a good worker . . . when you were around. The fastest typist I've ever seen. How does $4.50 an hour sound?"

It sounded like poverty and exploitation, but the only alternative was hunger, so I said, "Just fine. I'll be there in an hour."

I got dressed quickly and shut my left eye while I combed my hair. No use putting yourself in a bad mood when you need your enthusiasm for your work. As I drove into Stockton the back way, on Mariposa Road, a line from William Gass kept running over and over in my head. *From some ashes no bird rises.*

Ted's Typing Service is above San Joaquin County Suicide Prevention, which is above a tattoo parlor.

When I walked into the office, Faya looked at me and said, "Groovy."

"Groovy?" I thought *groovy* went out with the sixties.

"Your eye," she said and smiled. I guess she thought my eye was a political statement or a new fad. I wondered what drug she'd taken last.

Ted had a different opinion. "Sarah, my God, what happened to you?" He came up and gripped me by the upper arms and looked straight at me.

"I lost my eye," I said as calmly as I could. When in doubt, state the obvious in a calm voice.

"I'm sorry, Sarah, I'm really sorry, but I just don't think it would work." He let his hands drop to his sides, lowered his chin to his hollow chest.

"Don't think *what* would work?"

He looked at my eye for a moment and then nodded curtly.

Just then a customer walked in. She was around nineteen or twenty, perfect skin, bottled blond hair, carrying a term paper she wanted typed, probably from UOP. When she saw me she screamed, then turned around and ran.

"You get my point," Ted said, turning back to me.

"What about Gregory?" I said. "You let him work here and he has *AIDS!*"

"Yes, but that's different," Ted said in a careful voice. "You can't get AIDS from casual contact, so there's no real threat."

"You think you can lose an eye by looking at *this?*"

"No," he said, "but you could lose your breakfast."

Faya laughed. "I'm sorry," she said, laughing her guts out, "I'm really sorry. I really wish I could stop laughing"—here she nearly choked—"but I can't."

"What about a patch?" Ted asked. "Would you consider a patch? It would be unconventional but it wouldn't be so, uh . . ."

"No patch," I said. That's something I'd decided in the hospital. At the costume party of life I intended to go as myself.

"Well then, I'm sorry, Sarah, but I have to think of my customers."

"Your customers," I said. "Drunks and bums and an occasional college student?" In deference to their sensibilities I was not to be allowed to eat. It was not a view I could share wholeheartedly.

"You understand."

"No, I don't. And I'm not going to stand here smiling while you stick it to me."

"You're so *bitter,*" he said, dipping his chin again, moving his head backwards on his neck as if he'd just caught a whiff of something foul.

I said, "Look at this eye." I said, "If you're not bitter you haven't been paying attention."

"I'm sorry, Sarah. But if you change your mind about the patch . . ."

"I won't," I said and headed for the exit.

"Take care of yourself," Faya said. "Don't take any—"

I slammed the door on *wooden nickels.*

At the entrance to San Joaquin County Suicide Prevention I saw a hand-lettered sign that asked for hotline volunteers and I was tempted. I was that lonely.

When I got to the first floor I seriously considered a tattoo. Join the company of self-made freaks. I studied the pictures on the wall for quite a while. One woman had her shirt up over her breasts and her pants down to here, and her whole stomach was covered with a multi-colored ostrich, the tail ending up under her left armpit. Clearly this was intended as a personal statement of some sort, but who could tell what question it was the answer to?

∞

"WHAT'RE YOU TRYING TO DO you crazy fool—kill us all?" We were driving back from Stockton on Mariposa Road. We'd been to the horse races at the fair, then we'd hit the bars. It was Jake's car but Morgan was driving: Morgan wouldn't ride in a car he wasn't driving.

"You lose your freedom an inch at a time," he said calmly. "First you start driving the speed limit." He passed two more cars as I careened off the walls in the back seat. "The next thing you know you're doing what your boss tells you, showing up for work on time, bowing and scraping. Then your wife, you're listening to your God damn wife, for Christ's sake. Take out the garbage. Mow the lawn. Kiss me here." He pointed between his legs and he and Jake laughed. We barely made it past another car before an eighteen-wheeler blasted by, horn blaring, its wind rocking Jake's little green Maverick like a tuna can. "Before you know it, your life's over and it wasn't even your life." He turned his head in my direction in the dark of the car. I couldn't see his eyes but I knew what they looked like. "I'm not going to give that first inch," he said, just before the right tire blew.

This is the picture the insurance adjuster took after the crash. That's me there near the crushed hood ornament with my right arm in a cast.

"Hello?" Her voice sounded high and shallow, like a scared little girl's.

"What's the matter?"

"Sarah. Your brother has been charged with first-degree murder. They say he . . ."

"What? Tell me."

"I can't. It's too ugly even to say it, let alone believe it."

"Mom. Tell me."

"He . . . they say he . . . left her for the garbage men." She hesitated. "Naked."

"Who?"

"Arlene."

Arlene had been Morgan's third wife. Nobody in the family liked her. She was the kind of person who thought the history of human suffering was for her personal amusement. Stopped at a red light, she'd ask, "How many points?" whenever a disabled person was in the crosswalk. "Two? Three?" She was so beautiful that people stared in the streets, in restaurants, wherever she went. She had long black hair that she flung around like she was in a Nice 'n Easy commercial, large almond-shaped green eyes that made you think you were the single most important person on earth, and a body that would make a Playboy bunny sick with jealousy. Once when Arlene and I were at the Seven-11 picking up a six-pack, a guy who was himself no Nick Nolte said, so we could hear, "Beauty and the beast," which I did not appreciate but which gave Arlene a big lift. "I like it when men want me," she said. "You can't put it in the bank, but it sure beats indifference." Then she winked like she had a secret and was doing me a big favor to share it. Which apparently she had: she was sleeping with two state senators and a U.S. congressman while she was married to Morgan, which is why he divorced her. I understand, though, why he was deceived for so long. Someone that beautiful, you think they *must* have some inner goodness or special wisdom, something to justify such cosmic preferential treatment.

"Now look at her," I said and was ashamed.

"What?"

"Nothing. I was just thinking."

"Do you believe he's capable of something like that?"

When I thought of the way he tormented me and killed my twenty-six cats, I thought yes. When I thought of him as the person who stood beside me crying at the funeral by the edge of the creek, I thought no. We buried the cats in little shrouds—four or five to a gunnysack—and their going was witnessed by a fleet of small ships—walnut halves filled with wax, with a toothpick flag stuck into it, the name of a dead kitten printed on each flag. My mother taught us to make the boats to float in the bathtub. We stood together on the bridge, Morgan and I. He played taps on his trombone. Executioner *and* funeral director, he seemed to enjoy both parts and cried as loudly as I did.

"I don't know."

"Your father said he absolutely refused to believe it. Right after that he said, He's still family."

"What about Angela? What does she say?" Angela didn't have my bitterness about Morgan, since he never laid a hand on her. Maybe because she didn't provoke him. Or maybe he didn't have any energy left after trying to kill me.

"I haven't told her yet. You know how she reacts to . . . imperfection."

"Still, I think you should tell her. She has a right to know the truth."

"We come from a long line of truth-tellers," my mother said, getting sidetracked. "Except your grandmother Blight. You know I love her very much, and I know you don't like it when I say so, but she needed her crutch, she needed her illusions." Meaning God. As if God were a greater illusion than love.

"What's the truth? *We* don't even know the truth."

"That he's been arrested. We know that much," she said. "I just don't believe it. It's not a thing you think will ever happen in your own family. My sweet Morey."

"Can we go to visit him? Do they allow that?"

"Of course, they must. Even criminals have family," she said with the authority of reason in complete ignorance of the facts.

"Do you want to go with me? Maybe Angela would like to come too."

"You know I'd *like* to. I just don't know if I can." My mother, as I may have said, is afraid to leave her house. Afraid to go to the grocery store, afraid of crowds and open spaces. Afraid of many things. Sometimes I'm afraid it's only a matter of time until I become her, my life narrowed down to game shows and soap operas, sitting in one chair day after day.

"Let me know," I said, wanting to do something reckless, to prove I'm nothing like her, that as far as fear and trembling go, we're not even related.

"I will, honey. How are you doing? Your eye, I mean."

"Oh. Getting by."

"I love you, you know."

"I know." Having her on my side, it made me feel comforted, and I thought that Morgan, whatever he had done, needed us on his side.

"Mama?"

"What, honey?"

"What if it's true? If it's true, can you look at him the same ever again?"

"I don't know. I just don't know."

T HE WHITENESS OF HER BODY IS
what I saw first, a white movement beneath the trees, arms raised and
then lowered as in a dance. It was four in the morning. I had just come
home from a Swiss dance, drunk, in a good mood. I was in love with
Anthony D'Anado and he'd asked me to dance three times. I'd worn
my black crepe dress and three-inch high heels. I got out of the car
and staggered up the gravel driveway, but one of the heels broke.
That's when I saw her, hanging wash in the dark, naked.

"Mama?" I took off my shoes and walked toward her.

"Oh hi, honey."

"What are you doing?"

"I'm getting a jump on the wash."

"It's the middle of the night."

"Is it? Well, I couldn't sleep and I thought I might as well get a
head start."

"You don't have any clothes on."

She looked down at herself as if this were a surprise and then nodded. "I didn't want to disturb your father by opening and closing
drawers. And it's warm out." She held her arms out to her sides, palms
up, and smiled. "Did you have a good time?"

"I had a wonderful time."

"I'm glad, honey." She smiled at me again. "You should go to bed. It's late." She continued to bend and reach, bend and reach.

"What about you?"

"Oh, I'll just finish up here and then I'll be in." The clothes were mostly dark and they didn't show up against the night itself and it looked like a mime hanging the wash, my mother bending and reaching with nothing in her hands, nothing on the line, the quarter moon her only accompaniment.

"Good night, Mama."

"Good night, honey."

When I got up in the morning I said, "What were you doing hanging wash in the middle of the night?"

"Why I did no such thing," she said. "I was asleep in my bed the whole night. Ask your father."

He didn't look up from his newspaper. He wouldn't have noticed if the house burned down until it got to his eyebrows, or his whiskey ignited.

"I saw you," I said. I went out to point to the clothes but there were no clothes on the line.

The next time I caught her hanging wash in the middle of the night, I took this snapshot with Angela's Brownie Instamatic. For proof. Looking back, that was the real beginning of my career. It's striking, don't you think, the whiteness of her body, the movement of the trees?

THE PHONE RANG AND I GOT UP TO
answer it, thinking it might be Morgan, though I knew he was in jail.
But it was Richard, my ex-husband, calling from Kalispell, Montana.

"Can you meet me in Missoula?" Richard said. "There's something I want to talk to you about."

"About what?"

"About Sunny," he said.

The last time Sunny went to visit his father, at Christmas, before he went to Europe, he'd thrown him out. Because Sunny didn't want to chop wood before breakfast or go out drinking with him at night. Rich's idea of the good life. Sunny doesn't drink. What a disappointment. I was pissed off at Rich, that he couldn't cut his own kid some slack. But I didn't want to yell at him long distance.

"I've got to check a power station out west of there Friday morning," he said. "I'll get there Thursday and stay over Thursday night."

Today was Sunday. It's a hard drive, twenty-two hours from here, but I said, "Okay. I'll be there." It wasn't like I had to work or anything: I hadn't had a paying job since L.A. And I missed him. I hadn't seen him since Sunny's graduation from high school, three years ago. Every time I saw him I thought my life made sense. If your ex-husband still loves you, you can't be all bad. He's married again, but I figure he promised me Till-death-do-us-part first, so she's got nothing to complain about until the next life. Then he's all hers.

He gave me directions to the Crossbar Inn, at the west edge of town. He said he'd be in the bar by two, two-thirty.

"How will I recognize you?" I asked.

"By my face."

This was one of those exchanges that gets started and you can't remember how, and it doesn't really make any sense, but it's something we always said. Like "What a dump" (hitting the *t* and *p* hard), which we used to repeat whenever the house was a mess. Or "Fuck 'em, feed 'em fish," one of his favorites. Who knows where it comes from? But it gives you a history together, a language that leaves other people out.

Then it occurred to me that I should tell him. "I lost my right eye. It's pretty gruesome."

"Jesus Christ, Sarah, how did you do that? Are you all right?"

"It's a long sordid story. I just wanted to warn you. I'm not the perfect woman you married." I wanted to warn him not just for his sake but for mine. I didn't want him throwing up when he saw me, or falling off his barstool. A greeting like that would be hard to forget. And I couldn't afford to ruin any more of my past. Then I thought of telling him about Morgan. But I didn't. He'd never liked Morgan and this would just give him a chance to despise him with reason. And I didn't want anyone deciding whether he was guilty or innocent before I did.

"Jesus, sweetie, I'm sorry. Is there anything I can do?"

I said, "There *is* one thing . . ." and he laughed.

I looked at the clock. Ten A.M. I called the prison and got a recording that said visiting hours began at 1:00. I called Angela and told her I'd pick her up at noon. She was quiet on the phone, but I put it down to nerves. The prison was only ten minutes from the ranch, but I thought it might take a while to get my mother into the car, if the past was any evidence. I decided to pick up Angela first, so I'd have her help.

I was afraid to see Morgan in jail, afraid that it might change the way I thought of him—tall, arrogant, unhurtable. Being in jail makes people smaller. I know that because I used to go with Grandmother Blight to see Elsie in the women's prison in Stockton. Elsie was at least six-foot-two and weighed over three hundred pounds. I don't know what she was in prison for, but my grandmother visited her every week. The first time I saw her I cried because she looked so much smaller inside the cage. And she didn't tell her jokes anymore either. She lost her spark, my mother said.

I hoped Morgan would not shrink. "It's like a couch in a small room," my grandmother said. "It looks bigger. In a big room, though, like the visiting room at the prison, people look smaller. But they're still the same size." She looked at me carefully, bending her head down to my level, then said, "Elsie is made in God's image and likeness, so she's perfect. Do you understand that? Whatever God makes is perfect. Just like you and me." It was one of her standard speeches. I said, "Uh huh," but I didn't believe it. Weighing over three hundred pounds was not my idea of perfect. Neither was red hair, bow legs, and a nose that looks like it's been broken at the bridge.

On the way to get Angela I stopped to put gas in the car and considered calling my mother from the pay phone, but then thought it was better to take it for granted that my mother was going with Angela and me, instead of asking her and giving her the opportunity to back out. We could hold her hand if necessary, but I thought she should go to visit her own son in prison. It was a matter of loyalty. But would it be disloyal not to go if he'd really done it? Still, what good

was loyalty if it was yours only when you were on the side of goodness and righteousness, when the only time you could count on it was
when you didn't need it?

My mother used to lecture us kids when we were in high school:
"You're a Blight. And a Blight never does anything to dishonor the
Blight name." She never said what she had in mind, though I was
pretty sure getting pregnant or being thrown in the slammer for drunk
driving would qualify, both of which I accomplished by the age of
seventeen. "But there's nothing you can do that's so bad you have to
lie about it," she'd add, never telling us how the two things fit together.

I didn't believe Morgan had done that to Arlene, though I could
see how a person could. There's something about exceptional beauty
that makes you want to destroy it, to bring it down to your own level.
Awe is a hard attitude to maintain, especially when you yourself are
not pretty. Like Elsie in prison, it makes us small. Unless of course you
are deluded into thinking you are made in God's image and likeness,
like Arlene and Morgan. It was the one thing they had in common:
both of them thought they were God.

I tried to focus on Arlene, to remember her clearly, but she was a
blur of makeup and shiny black hair. Red lipstick. Long fingernails.
Only the details came back. She wore very short skirts and high heels.
See-through blouses that made men want her even before they looked
up into her face. It was hard to believe she was dead, someone that
infuriating. I think she thought of me as not quite human because I
wasn't beautiful. To Arlene, only the beautiful and the powerful really
existed. My brother had been powerful for a while, at least in our part
of California, and so she had wanted him. But there were other more
powerful men who had more money and she'd wanted them too.
Arlene was greedy. Maybe she thought that with her beauty and their
power she would never die. That's the thought I always had after

cutting the grass, making all the hedges clean and neat, sacking up the dead leaves: Now I'll live forever.

I turned on the radio to distract myself. Bonnie Raitt was singing, "Life isn't easy, love never lasts . . ."

I saw Jake's face in front of me, the calm blue eyes the exact color of my grandmother Blight's, the perfect white teeth, the dark skin. Before the picture could get a stranglehold on my heart, I mentally tied him up, with a stiff rope that twisted the black hairs on his ankles when I tightened the knot. I blindfolded him so I couldn't see his eyes. I pulled the gag—a red bandanna—a little tighter than necessary while I considered various kinds of sexual teasing, but finally concluded that this was not a thought worthy of the morally superior.

Right then I felt some sympathy for my brother and tried to think of some good memories, to give him at least a chance to be innocent in my mind.

My brother and I played together every day during our childhood. We built rafts out of fallen logs nailed together with two-by-fours and floated them down the creek. We rode horses and pretended to be a gang of desperadoes. I was Jesse James and Morgan was Billy the Kid. We caught calves in the barn and rode them backwards, holding on by the tail, and Grandfather Blight would come out and wave his red neckerchief at us and yell: "God damn it you little bastards, you'll make those calves *sway*backed!" Grandfather Blight was a hitter (ask Uncle Ad, who he treated like a punching bag), so we tried to stay out of his way, but being with my brother made me brave and I'd yell back, "Who cares if a God damn calf is swaybacked?" and we'd laugh loudly and keep on riding, until finally our grandfather would give up and go back inside the house. My brother liked to torture me, but I also think he loved me. Once I got my leg caught in a stanchion and it bled, and while we waited for my father to cross the field, he held my hand and said, "It will be all right."

When I drove up to my sister's house she came right out. She had on a white skirt and white blouse, an outfit I didn't think appropriate for going to visit someone in jail. I was wearing black.

She hugged me when she got into the car. "Oh Sarah," she said and then started to cry.

I held her in my arms and said, "Morey could not have done what they say he's done, even to Arlene. They'll discover their mistake sooner or later and everything will be back to normal." I spoke with great authority and her crying got quieter, then I patted her back and started the car. "It will all be straightened out by Thanksgiving. New Year's Eve at the latest," I said, which was when the whole family got together at the ranch, to look at Daddy's home movies for the past year, to see where we'd been. My mother made strawberry waffles and we all drank Ramos Fizzes. Then I said the lie I had remembered on the drive there: "It will be all right."

"Your eye," she said, indicating that she had been crying for me and not for our brother.

"Oh," I said, my heart dropping like a sack of dead cats.

I'd lost the radio station I'd been listening to, and we drove for a while in silence. When the silence became oppressive, I pushed in a Jennifer Warnes tape, "Famous Blue Raincoat," because I liked that wail in her voice. A hundred times in my life I had thought, If only I could sing. I wondered where Jennifer Warnes lived, alone or with someone, who she loved, if he loved her back, whether being able to sing like that protected her somehow, whether her family was as screwed up as mine was turning out to be. Maybe insanity, like the ability to sing, was hereditary.

I looked over at my sister. Her face was pale, no makeup, and her long blond hair was pulled back. She's a year older than I am but right then she looked about twelve. Her hands were folded in her lap too neatly and it worried me, like she was trying to will some order into the universe by body English alone.

"Angela," I said, and when she looked at me she started to cry again. I didn't know whether it was for me or my brother or for something else, something in her own life.

I said, "Go ahead, scream your head off," but she immediately went quiet, as if so much personal attention had killed her grief. "How are you doing?" I asked, putting my free hand on hers. The tops of her hands were getting small brown spots, but the moons of her fingernails were perfect halfmoons.

"Fine," she said, like she always did. Angela was the kind of person who thought you could never complain, even when your leg was dying of gangrene and your husband was hitting you and your kids were selling cocaine. To express herself she drew cartoons. She had this character named Marjorie Morningstar. One cartoon I especially liked was of a woman on a cliff with the caption, "Marjorie Morningstar edges closer and closer to a complete nervous breakdown." Another one had a woman waking up frightened (big saucer eyes and the lines coming out from her head like the ones they draw on a lightbulb) beside her husband. It said, "Marjorie Morningstar faces reality." I told her she ought to sell them to a newspaper, get them syndicated, or collect them together into a book. But she said she didn't have time, taking care of a husband and three kids. So let them take care of themselves, I'd say, and that would be the end of that conversation. This was the principle upon which my sister and I parted ways.

We stopped at a red light in Manteca and a woman crossed the street in front of us, with scraggly long gray hair, the kind that looks like a dirty string mop, with the shoes rotting off her bony white feet. She was sixty-five, maybe, pushing a shopping cart filled with paper bags, a blanket, junk. In one corner was a pink and orange plaid teddy bear with both eyes gone. I immediately put my hand up to my good eye to see if it was still there. When the woman got halfway across she turned around and stared straight at me. She had small dark eyes in a ruined face, fierce as a weasel's. I wanted to tell her I didn't do it. I wanted to give her the cheese sandwich I'd eaten yesterday for lunch. What did she expect of me? I didn't run the world. Maybe I should have invited her home, let her sleep on my floor. Then again, maybe she liked where she was now better than wherever she had left, whatever she called her life before the money ran out. Probably she told her boss off one time too many. She hadn't learned that compromise is necessary for living in the world. If I didn't get another job soon, I'd probably end up the same way, with someone looking me over at a crosswalk with a feeling of pity and shame. I was glad I had my camera with me. I wanted to keep that face.

I drove through the tall wooden arch made from railroad ties with our name carved into it—Blight—that my brother had built at the entrance to my parents' driveway. The gravel road was filled with ruts and mud puddles, and the weeping willows, I noticed, needed to be cut back over the bridge. I could hear the branches crack as I drove over it, a sound like bones breaking. I thought of Arlene.

I honked the horn as I drove up to my mother's house. The creek was still there, the saltgrass hills and the oak trees, but something had changed. For a moment I studied the scene, which had become invisible by being too familiar.

My brother's red Maserati was missing. He'd spent half his time over here and its absence left a hole.

I saw my mother pull back the drapes in the picture window and peer out. I waved and smiled but her eyes did not look relieved to see who it was. She closed the drapes back over her face.

"Let's go in for a few minutes," I said to Angela. "Have a cup of coffee and help her on with her coat."

We walked into the hall where my mother was standing rigid under the three swallows on the wall, near the door chimes. I thought of the song, "When the Swallows Come Back to Capistrano," but I couldn't remember what happened when they came back. Did they come home to die? Was it a love song? Right then I got a mental picture of Jake cutting up vegetables for his Italian soup and I felt like someone had delivered a karate-chop to my neck, brought me to my knees.

"I can't go," my mother said. Her eyes were rolled back, all whites, and she was breathing funny. Shallow, panting, like a winded dog.

"Mom, we'll be right here with you. Nothing is going to happen." When I said that, she backed up and kept on backing until she was in the living room, sitting in the rocker. I noticed Daddy wasn't there. There was no sign of his whiskey glass on the end table.

"Where's Daddy?" I asked.

She didn't answer.

"Where's Daddy?"

She said, "I'm sorry. I thought I could go but I can't." Her mouth was screwed up like a stroke victim's. "Tell Morey I tried. I really tried."

"I wouldn't call this trying," I said, deciding to get tough. It had worked the last time, the day she'd promised to go to my graduation from Modesto J. C. That was when I was thirty. God, she hadn't been off this ranch for nearly ten years. Going from living room to kitchen to bedroom to bath, over and over, nothing new under the sun. Watching TV and reading her throat-slitting poetry and smoking un-filtered Camels to show that living was not something she placed much value on.

When she didn't budge I went over and put my arm around her shoulder, took her hand. "Come on, you can do it," I said, helping her up.

Angela held her other hand. "Come on, Mama, we're right here with you. There's nothing to be afraid of."

"Breathe evenly, keep calm, we're walking to the car now," I said, taking her by the elbow while Angela engineered her other side. There was a hole in the bottom of the front door I hadn't noticed when I came in. It looked like someone had put a boot through it. I wanted to ask what had happened but I thought it unwise to mention it right then.

When she got to the car she went rigid and started grabbing for us as if we weren't right there. "I can't!" she said. "I just can't!" She was breathing fast. "I feel like the world is spinning and spinning and I'm going to slip off." Her hands were clammy and her face was covered with little beads of sweat. I was afraid she was going to have a heart attack.

"It's okay," I said. "You don't have to go. It's okay. Relax."

She smiled at me then and her breathing abruptly changed. Living was once more possible.

"Are you ashamed of me?" she asked in a voice not of shame but of relief. "I'm ashamed of myself."

"No, Ma, we're not ashamed of you," I said, but my voice could not have been very convincing. I was disgusted with all the effort gone toward getting her into the car and there she stood. But her gray hair was turned blond by the light through the leaves of the oak tree and it made me feel softer toward her.

"You tried," Angela said and smiled. "That's the important thing. You got all the way out to the car. We'll tell Morey you did your best. He'll be proud of you." Angela was the diplomat. If you weren't going to succeed at something, why add to the world's misery by being ashamed as well, leaving aside the thought that perhaps some things were worthy of shame.

My mother smiled, a guilty yet triumphant smile, like a kid who's stolen candy but is known to have leukemia.

We walked her slowly back into the house and sat her down in the rocking chair, clicked on the TV for her, helped her prop up her feet, lit her a cigarette.

Jeopardy was on and the host was giving an answer no one knew the question to. "Played Stanley Kowalski in *A Streetcar Named Desire*."

The buzzer sounded louder than usual and I felt like it was for us.

"Marlon Brando!" my mother yelled. "Who is Marlon Brando?! Where do they get these people anyway? Dumb as doornails." She looked up at Angela and me and rolled her eyes, settled once again into her accustomed chair, drapes drawn, all the light outside the window, dragging on her unfiltered Camel, safe at last.

THE JAIL MY BROTHER WAS BEING
held in is just outside Manteca, near Sharpe's Depot, a huge gray
structure on top of a hill, made of stone. It was built by someone
whose name I forget, as an experiment in prison reform. There is a
tall observation tower in the center of the quad, in which the guards
are hidden from the prisoners' view, while the open-barred cells
below form a circle around it, about thirty feet back, making con-
stant surveillance both possible and unnecessary. I'd been in it once
before, on a 4-H field trip. It had given me the feeling, even as a vis-
itor, that the unseen figures in the tower were the zookeepers and
we were the zoo. The belief that you are being constantly watched
makes you into something low, as if you had no unknown motives, no
inner life.

My brother was on that field trip too. The guard showed us what
looked like a gas chamber in a room at the base of the stone steps, and
all the other children cowered and whimpered and cried for their
mothers, except my brother: he walked across the room and sat in the
high-backed chair, strapping himself in, his laughter echoing in the
dungeon-like room. That was a day I admired him.

This is a picture of Morgan sitting in the lifeguard station he made of railroad ties that stood at the end of the swimming pool. No one else was allowed to sit in it, on pain of mutilation and early death. Sometimes I would tiptoe outside in the middle of the night and sit there shivering in my thin white nightgown.

WHEN I FIRST SAW MORGAN HE was dressed in blue things like pajamas and he was not as big as I'd remembered. There was a glass wall covered with a wire screen between us and we had to take turns talking on a telephone that had what looked like what I hoped was chocolate smeared over the mouthpiece.

Angela picked up the phone first. "I'm so sorry," she said and then started to cry. All the while Angela was crying and talking I studied Morgan's hands, as if by simply staring I could see the memory of blood, and know for sure what they had or had not done to Arlene. I watched his mouth moving and heard muffled sounds through the glass wall and it had a ludicrous effect, like watching the TV with the sound off, like a mime playing charades to save his life.

Morgan caught me staring and looked quickly away, put his hands, palms together, between his thighs.

"How are they treating you?" I asked when I got my turn, trying to sound cheerful.

"All the comforts of home," he said and made a sweeping gesture with his hand. "What the hell happened to your eye?"

"A slight accident," I said. "With a pool cue." I tried to smile.

"Any offers from the circus yet?" he asked, then laughed his big-boom laugh.

I started to cry, to slobber into the phone.

"Jesus Christ, don't start bawling. I was just kidding."

"This is my *face*," I said. "It's not funny."

He didn't say he was sorry but he did the thing closest to it for him—he changed the subject. "Where's Mom and Daddy? Aren't they coming?"

"Mom wanted to, but you know how she is. She only made it to the car and started having a panic attack. She wanted you to know she tried." I noticed a strong smell of urine and sweat and fear. I wanted to leave.

"Yeah," he said bitterly. "Just like she tried to come to my graduation."

I looked at him, a forty-three-year-old man who held it against his mother sick with an honest-to-God mental disorder for not coming to his high school graduation. Now there's a talent for grudge-keeping.

"What?" he asked.

"Oh, nothing. Just thinking. *Dad*. You asked about Daddy. I haven't seen him in days. He must be trying to get you a lawyer or hire a private detective or something. Get you out of here." I made my eyes wide, full of false hope, and bobbed my head up and down.

"I know people," he said. "They owe me. I can get my own dick." He raised his head in contempt and for a moment he was his old self, swaggering in his chair. "I'll be out of here by tonight." Big deep laugh. "Bet your ass."

"Well, good," I said. I had not known, until that moment, that I didn't believe him—didn't believe in his innocence or possibly even his existence. His power must have come in part from fear. It made him seem bigger than life. But now that he couldn't do any more damage than to hurt my feelings, he'd shriveled, like firecracker worms on the fourth of July.

"How's my loyal wife?" he asked.

Morgan's fourth wife was Leona Marie. They'd only been married a year and from the sound of the yelling coming from across the creek, I didn't think it would last one more. I wondered, though, who would take care of Morgan's two boys if she left him. Maybe he'd have to do it himself.

"Hasn't she come to see you?"

"No," he said. "The bitch probably believes I did it."

"You didn't," I said, not in the tone of a question. I lowered my head, ashamed of my disloyalty, having ceased to believe in my brother in spite of the fact that I had no evidence. For whatever reason—the ridiculous blue pajamas, the way he moved his hands, eyes that darted and strayed, lacking conviction, the too-hearty laugh—I had shut my heart against him, slammed the door. But I vowed not to let anyone know it, not even Angela. I owed him that.

"Thanks," he said, but I couldn't tell if his voice was mean or neutral or if he really meant it.

There was an announcement over the loudspeaker that visiting hours were over.

"Gotta go," Morgan said, as if his public were calling. "Take it easy. Or any way you can get it."

Same old jokes. "Goodbye," I said. "We'll see you . . ." I left it dangling because I didn't know when we would see him.

"In hell," he said and laughed.

I looked back on my way out the door but he was already gone. Instead I caught the eye of a prisoner who was just going through the door. He was about three hundred pounds, three hundred pounds of

flesh straining against the thin blue material; his face looked like someone had blown it up with a bicycle-tire pump and it was about to
explode. He made a circle with the thumb and middle finger of his
left hand, then put the middle finger of his right hand through the circle, over and over, smiling fiendishly.

When Angela and I got into the car she turned to me and said,
"What do you think?" She was no longer tearful.

"What do I think about what?"

"Did he do it?"

"Angela." I looked at her dead-eyed. "He's our brother."

"Well, I'm not going to be Miss Marjorie Morningstar this time.
Maybe he did. He's mean enough to enjoy hurting anyone who stood
in his way, and we both know it."

"Where's Daddy?" I asked, to change the subject. "He wasn't
there this morning when we went to get Mom."

"I don't know. I haven't seen him since—let's see—a week ago
last Tuesday, when I was over there for dinner. Come to think of it,
nobody said much the whole time except Mama, and then only to
me."

"Something's fishy," I said. "Something's going on."

She didn't answer me but I knew it was true. The human body is
like a thermometer: high anxiety means trouble in the world.

"There is no life, truth, intelligence, nor substance in matter. All
is infinite Mind and its infinite manifestation, for God is All-in-all.
Spirit is immortal Truth; matter is mortal error. Spirit is the real and
eternal; matter is the unreal and temporal. Spirit is God, and man is
His image and likeness. Therefore man is not material; he is spiritual."
Angela whispered the words to herself.

I didn't believe any of it but it soothed me. It was like having
Grandmother Blight there beside me, reading The Daily Lesson. I

hadn't realized until then how much I missed her, considered her dead. She had a few short circuits in her brain but she wasn't dead. I hoped I didn't end up like that—great body, no mind. Then I laughed: it was what we'd wanted most in high school, so the boys would like us.

"What's so funny?" Angela said.

I didn't want to explain it to her. I knew it would sound callous if not cruel, so I told her about the three-hundred-pound guy I saw on our way out of the prison, what he'd done with his hands, the fiendish light in his eyes.

"That's disgusting," she said. "I wish you hadn't told me that. Now I'll never be able to get the image out of my mind."

"I'm sorry."

"It's all right," she said, and then she looked straight ahead, folded her hands in her lap, lowered her head, and I saw her lips moving again, heard her whispering. "The Lord Thy God my Master is, His goodness faileth never. I nothing lack for I am His, and He is mine forever."

THAT'S ME ON THE FLOOR. MORGAN is on top of me, his knees pinning my shoulders, the heels of his hands on my wrists.

"Say 'Master.'"

I shook my head.

He began to drool, the string of spit hanging down within an inch of my face, him slurping it up just before it fell.

"Say 'Master.'"

"No," I said, sticking my chin out and raising up slightly on my elbows for emphasis.

He sat on my head (so I couldn't lean toward him and away from the pain) and pulled my hair.

"Say 'Master.'"

"No!"

He turned me over and twisted my arm up behind my back. I heard several sharp crunches, a symphony of bones.

"Say 'Master.'"

"Uh-uh."

In my memory I never gave in.

My grandmother Blight be-
lieved that we live again. This is not the only life. No, this is not life at
all; it is error, illusion. Real life awaits us.

Maybe that's why I went to see her, to study her face in the dark,
to contemplate the possibility of a new and better life without the
body to hold us down. I hadn't gone to visit her since the accident.
That's how I thought of it—the accident—though I knew it was no
accident but a consequence of the way I had been living my life.

Grandmother Blight is in the Wayside Nursing Home, in Manteca, a ten-minute drive from the ranch. The nursing home is clean,
decorated in southwest colors, the floors scrubbed and shined. Everyone is friendly in a way that seems genuine, even in the Bingo room.
The policy of the home is that visitors can come whenever they want
to, a policy that inspires confidence that you have chosen the right
place for a loved one: they have nothing to hide. There is another policy, however, that has caused some trouble for my grandmother. Each
resident must have a "doctor of record," someone to call in case of
emergency. This is the possibility that horrified my grandmother all
her life—that she would fall and hit her head or otherwise be ren-
dered unconscious and be taken to a hospital against her will, tubes
stuck into her, operations performed, procedures that assaulted her

dignity and her disbelief in worldly medicine.

Most of the time when I went to visit her she was propped in a wheelchair with the television on. She never watched TV when she lived in the house where Morgan lives now, and being propped staring at it seemed surrealistic. But I thought I knew why they did it: to give the death house the sounds of life, the rise and fall of arguments, music, human voices. She never played Bingo before this either, and does not know the rules. Every time they called a number, she would look under the red chips she had already put down, as if the winning number might be hiding. She had lucid moments now and then, when she knew who I was and could comment on her predicament: "T'ain't funny, McGee." Then she'd laugh, shake her head, her spirit intact. Or perhaps she only seemed lucid, and the phrases she repeated were always appropriate.

This was the first time I had ever come in the middle of the night. There was no one at the reception desk. I walked down the scrubbed halls with the lights at knee-level to guide the way. I punched the UP arrow at the elevator, and got out on the fourth floor. I went into her room, opened the curtains slightly so the moon would shine on her face. I got a chair from the other side of the room and sat it by her bed. I put my hands through the bars of the bed-guard, held her hand. She is eighty-seven, but she had always looked young, her skin as smooth as a woman of forty. She was sleeping with her mouth slightly open, her neck bent at an odd angle, as if she were in great pain. Unable to move easily now, she stayed in the position in which she was left on being moved from wheelchair to bed. I tried to straighten her out without waking her.

"Everything I believed . . ." I stopped, not knowing what came next. She snored slightly in response, and I began to sing, an old hymn from childhood.

Shepherd, show me how to go,
o'er the hillside steep,
how to gather, how to sow,
how to feed Thy sheep.
I will listen for Thy voice,
lest my footsteps stray.
I will follow and rejoice,
all the rugged way.

I rocked and hummed and held the flat bone of her wrist for an hour
or more. Her skin looked like wax in the moonlight when I clicked
the shutter, but her sleeping face was beautiful.

Each time I came I tried to vividly imagine her life before this
place, to resurrect some good memory, so that the power of her per-
sonality and mind during eighty-some years would not be displaced
by the sickness of the last few months.

She offers me diet Coke and storebought chocolate chip cookies
which I accept but do not eat. I sit on her green brocade couch; she
sits in the swivel chair by the dusty closed drapes. She is, oh, sixty, I'd
say, and she still lives in the house where Morgan lives now.

"Why don't you open those up?" I always ask. "Let in some light?"

She smiles but offers no defense of the dark.

"You look good," she says. "You must be happy."

"Yes," I say. The truth is too complicated to know where to bend
it so I just lie.

"Happy," she repeats, nodding her head. She has a noble face —
high forehead, prominent cheekbones, large blue eyes — that despite
her age has not fallen.

"What have you been doing?"

"As many as I can," she says. "The easy ones twice."

This is a vulgar saying that she uses often but does not understand. But she laughs when she says it, so I'm never sure.

She tells the same stories again and again. She took Uncle Ad to the World's Fair in Seattle when he was very young. She is unsure of the year. They went up there on the bus, but (this was to be a great surprise) came back on a plane. He had never ridden on an airplane before and the excitement made him giddy and obnoxious. He was running up and down the aisle asking people for their peanuts and my grandmother had to go after him.

"Is that your son?" an older woman asked.

"No," my grandmother said, "he's my nephew." Here she interjects a commentary, a slight frown. "I lied," she says. "I lied and I don't know why. It's something I've always regretted."

I nod, place my hand on top of hers to show we all have regrets.

Comforted, she continues. "My, what a handsome young man, the woman said, and gave him her bag of peanuts. But Ad threw it on the floor with the other six bags he had managed to cadge and ran back to his seat. When I got back and sat down beside him, he asked, Why didn't you claim me? Why didn't you *claim me?*" Her voice rises when she gets to this part, his grief fixing the timbre, as if she knew what it felt like to be him.

"He wanted me to say that I was his mother," she says, her hands altering the dusty light around us as she speaks. "He wanted me to say that he belonged to me. He did, of course. He always did. But he needed to be told it."

My grandmother tells this story over and over because she needs to believe that Uncle Ad did not kill himself because he thought no one loved him.

Every time after hearing it I wonder, What stories do I tell over and over, what do I need to believe?

"He knew you loved him," I whispered, though I didn't remember saying it at the time.

Before leaving, I kissed her on the cheek, wondering how long she would last, and whether in her case longer was better. It is so difficult to die at the right time.

On my way out I passed the music room, and there was an old woman sitting at the organ, staring at her hands poised above the keys. I had an impulse to go in, to say something, to remind her of what she meant to do.

I looked at the clock over the elevator. Almost six a.m. I pushed the DOWN arrow.

"Good morning, Miss Blight," a woman in white said as she passed me in the hall, smiling. "Mr. Meese." She nodded toward my companion. "I see you've brought your camera with you today, Miss Blight. Taking snapshots of Grandma, are we?"

I looked at her closely in an attempt to detect some insincerity. Finding none, I said, "Good morning."

A small man in a dark gray suit looked me over. His eyes were light blue, the color of nonfat milk, and he had the kind of nose you get from drinking too much: red, bloated, pores large enough for a small animal to live in.

"I guess you're wondering what someone with one eye looks like," I said and offered him an understanding smile as the doors sucked closed in front of us.

He jerked himself away as if I'd asked him to do something unseemly.

"I *said,* I guess you're wondering what someone with one eye looks like. You can look if you want to. I don't mind in the slightest."

He moved as close as possible to the gray metal doors. His nose was nearly touching them, so anxious was he to get out of this small moving room with the one-eyed freak in it.

"Though you'd probably like to think so, I'm not much different from you," I said casually, touching his shoulder. He had, I noticed, a bad case of dandruff.

"Do not *touch* me!" he spit. "Do. Not. Touch. Me." This time he made each word a sentence. I peered around his gray shoulder and I could see his face fill with terror, I could hear his blood scream. Get me *outta* here! This woman is a nut! This woman is a lunatic!

When the elevator doors started to open, he pried them apart with his fingertips and scurried out so fast he tripped on his own shoes. He looked back up at me with a frown as if I were responsible for this too.

I showed him my empty hands, shrugged my shoulders: No tricks, honest. But this did nothing to allay his suspicions. He hurried off to his scared wife and their three timid children. In the full-length mirror between the two sets of elevator doors I could see him getting smaller and smaller, and I tried to predict the point at which he would disappear.

That's when I saw it: my eye, in close-up. I saw it the way he must have seen it, and it came as a shock and a fresh horror. He was afraid of me because of my eye! I clicked the shutter as my face registered the thought that I was no longer homely; I now had the capacity to terrify.

WE HAVE A SHARED MEMORY, MY brother and I, of an event we never witnessed. Our Uncle Addison's funeral. We weren't allowed to attend because my mother said we were too little—I was five and Morgan was nine—but we can both describe the details. The way the room looked, with the casket in front, the exact colors of the stained glass window behind the minister's head—indigo and red and little leaves of green— with Jesus on the cross, a halo of thorns. The wreath of carnations that hung on a wooden frame like an easel, the way they slid in a half circle toward the casket after the minister finished his sermon, as if Uncle Addison were trying to give us a sign. How this old woman in a purple dress with a quavery voice sang "Nearer My God to Thee" and "The Old Rugged Cross" and "Shepherd Show Me How to Go," and everyone cried except Aunt Martha. What his face looked like—all powdery and pale—though neither of us had seen a person's face in death. The clean and newly clipped fingernails, though Uncle Addison's fingernails were never clean because he worked in the garage most evenings. My mother said we must have heard the relatives talking about it at the house, after the funeral, when everyone came over for potluck. But even people who see the same accident tell different stories, so I don't believe that could be right. It was a puzzle I had contemplated on and off for the thirty-some years since Uncle Addison died: came home from the Korean war, found Aunt Martha pregnant with another man's child, swallowed a grenade like the ones he'd used on "them," then patiently waited for his death to bloom inside him.

This is an ordinary snapshot of fireworks on the fourth of July, but it brings back the memory that has no photograph to keep its place. There I am with the lit sparkler in my long red hair, the one Morgan carefully set in order to light up the night while waiting for the grand finale. There is the smell of burning hair, that slight crackle. The second shot is of me screaming, my mouth the perfect O of Saturday cartoons. The halo around my head in the third frame is a fire that left me bald and my eyebrows singed but caused no lasting damage. I don't know who the photographer was, but if you flip through the snapshots very quickly, they seem to move.

At first I hoped the letter was from Jake, saying he still loved me and wanted to come home. He'd walked out many times before, and had always come back, with a story good enough that someone with Alzheimer's might believe it. But when I saw the title I knew it was from Sunny.

Ever since Sunny left home, at the age of seventeen after a bitter fight with his father, he'd written me letters with titles. I've saved them all. The first, the one at the top of the stack tied in red ribbon, is *Non Serviam*. The one at the bottom is titled *I-Broke-My-Fist-for-Love-of-You Blues*. The titles alone, in their original order, tell a story.

I don't know where he got the idea—that a title somehow gave a plain letter dignity or interest or added meaning, something it didn't have on its own. Perhaps it was from the example of my titled photographs. But whatever the explanation was, I took these letters, this meager evidence, as a sign that I had been a good mother. He wanted to keep talking to me. He knew I would listen. He knew I would always love him. Even if.

L'histoire des Choses Vertes qui Sautent

When I first got here I tried not to be an Ugly American.
I kept my door closed, my legs covered, my voice down. I ate
things you can find in swamps, without complaint. I was peeved
to see American fast food places where you don't even have
to speak French, and English was all over, words like "hot dog,"
"week-end," "T-shirt."

Now I use those words whenever possible and wear my
tennis shoes and Gurkha shorts to the *Place de la Republique*
every Saturday to shout, *"Vive l'Amerique!"* from the top of
the monument.

O France: haute couture, haute cuisine, *accents circonflexes,*
soirees, patisseries, French bread, gangs of adolescent punks with
leather jackets and slicked-back hair.

Everyone told me that a year abroad would change my life, but
I thought my transformation would come in the form of a tall, cool
French woman who could lift one eyebrow to call a cab.

No.

I should say here that though I do not look at all French,
people always stop me to ask directions. Perhaps what distinguishes
me from French people also attracts lost people.

So, walking along the rue de Fleurus that day, I thought the
three guys in the car were asking directions, and I turned around.

The one on the passenger side said, "Are you homosexual?"
With a credible accent. (It was probably the only English sentence
he knew, so it got a lot of use.)

I didn't know much French then, but I could say "little frog,"
so I did: "No, but you can suck my dick anyway, *petite grenouille."*

He became enraged—perhaps he knew more English than I gave him credit for—and grabbed the wheel. The horn blared, the car mounted the curb, and I was knee-to-bumper with a '78 Peugeot.

I put my backpack on the ground and calmly rummaged through it. When my attacker came bounding toward me I shot him, right between the eyes, with the pistol that I carry for such purposes. Then, because I'm not the kind of guy to leave things unfinished, I shot the other two, and took their leather jackets as trophies. Then I went to McDonald's.

O Mom. The world is ugly, and the people are sad.

Sunny

"He's not here," she said in the voice you use for someone who is trying to sell you something you don't want.

"When is he coming back?"

"I don't know."

"What do you mean you don't know?"

"Just what I said, Sarah. I don't know." Her voice was narrow-eyed and tight-lipped.

"What happened? Did you two have a fight?"

"Yes. We had a fight."

"What about?"

"About none of your business."

"Mom."

"Okay, it was about Morey. I said I didn't believe he did it. Your father was of another opinion. We passed the matter back and forth for a day or two, and then I said if he could believe that of our son, I didn't want him in my bed. I didn't want to sleep with a traitor."

"Where did he go?"

"I don't know. Maybe he's at the Motel 6 in town. It's about as far as his imagination would take him."

"How long has he been gone?"

"Two weeks," she said. "He put his boot through the front door on the way out. A nice last touch, I thought." I could see her smiling to herself, admiring her sense of irony.

"What are you going to do?"

"I'm doing it," she said. I could picture her sitting there smoking and watching TV, clicking from one channel to the next, reading her uplifting poetry during commercials. Her favorites now were Sylvia Plath and Anne Sexton.

"Aren't you going to try to find him?"

"What good would that do?"

I thought about this for a moment. I didn't know. But it seemed to me that if two members of your family couldn't agree on whether their son had humiliated and killed another human being, a human being he had promised to love and cherish forever, something was very wrong. But it was something that could be fixed with the right words and a little goodwill.

Picturing her there in that chair made me feel some sympathy for her. "Are you scared there all by yourself?" I asked. "I could come."

"No, honey, I'm fine," she said. "It's people that scare me, not being alone."

"Do you want me to try to find him?"

She didn't say anything for a while. "No." Her voice was neutral, as if she'd fully considered it. "You know what he said? He said that Morey did it. He said he had irrefutable evidence." She made the word "irrefutable" sound like what it meant.

"What evidence?"

"I don't know," she said. "I didn't ask. When he's drinking you can't reason with him, I don't even try. You know that little worm-like vein in his forehead? Well, it was throbbing. That's when I shut up. I just shut my mouth."

I wanted to know the evidence. I wanted to see it with my own eyes. Eye. "Mom?"

"What, honey?"

"Do you think it's possible?"

"No, I don't," she said with conviction. "In my experience, anything your father believes is probably false."

"Do you think Arlene deserved it? Not saying he did it, but if he did, would she have deserved it?"

"Arlene was a little slut."

In our family, "little slut" is a term of affection. So I was surprised my mother chose that word. It made Arlene seem more human, more part of our family. A person with flaws, yes, but our flawed sister, not a dead stranger.

"Did she deserve to be killed?" my mother asked. "No," my mother said. "I don't think she did. I don't think anyone deserves to lose her life just because she can't please a man."

When I hung up I started calling the motels in Manteca. I found Daddy on the sixth try, at the Golddust Inn. I asked the clerk to ring his room, but there was no answer.

I got my keys and purse, went out and started the car. If Daddy wasn't in the motel he'd be in the closest bar. Some things in life you can count on.

I thought of my father sitting alone in a dark bar. Sometimes, before I moved into Uncle Ad's house, I would get up in the middle of the night for a glass of water. I'd walk down the hall, trying to be quiet, and go into the kitchen. That's when I'd see the yellow light from the swag lamp in the living room, and my father sitting in the big leather chair, a glass in his hand, the sound on the TV turned clear down, the images from the screen flashing on his face like the shifting light of an ambulance.

I'd go in and sit beside him in my mother's chair.

"Hi, Daddy," I'd say, like this was normal, drinking in the dark in the middle of the night, watching TV with the sound off.

"Hi, honey," he'd say. "What time is it?"

"It's late, Daddy. You should go to bed." Then I'd get up to look at the kitchen clock. "Three A.M."

"I've been thinking," he'd say. "I've been thinking what a good life I've had. I can't complain."

Whenever he started saying what a good life he'd had, I knew he was sad, I knew there was something he couldn't face.

"A good life," he'd say again, holding up his glass in the dark. "I've done everything I wanted to do. Except go down to the bottom of the Grand Canyon on a donkey. That's something I haven't done."

"Well, why not? Why not do it?"

"Your mother can't get along without me for that long."

That was always his excuse. My mother. What would she do without him to do her grocery shopping, to buy her books, to empty her ashtray.

"I could take care of her. Angela and I could."

"She depends on me. She likes to know someone's looking out for her."

I nodded. "Okay, Daddy. No Grand Canyon."

"Still, I've had a wonderful life. I own this land. There are people who would kill for a beautiful spread like this. Just last week I had a guy over in Farmington tell me it was the most beautiful place in the valley."

"It is, Daddy."

"I haven't been sick a day in my life," he said, tapping his chest with the tips of his fingers. "And I've been lucky to have a wonderful woman like your mother for my wife."

"Yes, Daddy, you've been lucky." Waiting on an agoraphobic all your life, someone who can't go anywhere with you because she can't leave her house, now there's a piece of luck. Bad, I thought, and then felt mean.

As if he'd been thinking the same thing, he said in her defense, "Your mother and I, we used to go dancing five nights a week. I'd have liked to go every night, but she said she needed a rest. Five nights a week. I was never happier than I was then. We used to go to the ballroom in Tracy. Five nights a week." He smiled to himself, remembering.

I thought of my mother getting ready to go out, her rituals. She'd start with a bubble bath, and invite me in to sit and talk to her. That was the time I felt closest to her, when she was in her bubble bath and the air was warm and full of the excitement and possibility of a good time. She'd ask me what I thought she should wear. "The red dress?" she'd say. "Or the pale blue?" And whatever I chose, that's what she'd wear. She said I was her advisor. "Everyone needs an advisor," she'd add. Then when she got out of the tub, she'd put Jergen's lotion all over her body, rubbing the excess into her hands, and then a little for mine, rubbing my hands between hers. After she put talcum powder on her breasts, she'd slip into her white silk robe while I held it for her. She wore this robe to put on her makeup. My mother was beautiful. She had green eyes and auburn hair, very thick. She put on her makeup in front of a mirror with little lights all around it. I watched her carefully: liquid makeup on her face, rouge, then eyebrow pencil, finally coloring her lips, making sure she didn't go outside the lines. In that bathroom, when she was getting ready to go out dancing with my father—those were the times I felt safe.

I wondered what had happened to scare her so badly that she couldn't leave her house anymore. I'd never asked her. Maybe it was no one thing, just a suspicion that grew. She'd been like that for so long now that we thought of it as—not normal exactly but just the way things were. Like Daddy's drinking. A fifth of Chivas Regal a day. "A fifth a day'll keep the doctor away," Daddy said. Then he'd laugh. Old Doc Watson told him he should quit, said his liver was twice the normal size. But Doc Watson was a drunk too, so it didn't have much force. Like someone trembling and at the same time telling you there's nothing to be afraid of. You don't believe it.

"I'm tired, Daddy," I'd say finally. "I just got up for a drink of water."

"Okay, honey. It was nice talking to you." He always said that, as if we had just met at a party and this was his gracious way of taking leave. Thinking of this made me cry.

My father was sitting at the bar with a fifth of Chivas in front of him. He must've already made friends with the bartender. The camcorder was next to the bottle, its little red light glowing in the dark.

It took my eye a moment to adjust. Being in the Sea Horse brought it all back: the pool cue, the assault, Jake sitting there calmly watching me be mutilated. I started to cry again. Lately weeping seemed to be my natural state. My father came over to me, put his arm around me.

"Daddy," I said, and he looked surprised. So he would've helped me even if I weren't his daughter. There was something heartening in that.

"What's the matter, honey? What are you doing here?" Then he saw it, even in the dark. "Jesus, baby, what happened to your eye?"

"Didn't Mom tell you? I thought Mom would tell you."

"Maybe she did, honey, but I—" He held up his drink.

"I got it put out. With a pool cue. Last January."

He looked at me for a long time without saying anything, as if the truth were not a good enough explanation.

I said, "It's still me."

He patted me on the back and sat me down on the barstool next to him. "It's still you," he repeated, nodding, but his voice lacked conviction.

"That's not why I came to find you," I said. "Mom said you had evidence. Evidence that Morey . . . did what they say he did. I need to know."

His eyes in the dark bar were coming into focus and I saw that they had fear in them. His head was hunkered down over the glass of golden whiskey and he looked like the fugitive on that TV show. I think I always watched that show to see what would happen to my father next. They had the same face. The same kind, self-effacing manner that made you want them to get away. To escape.

But then my thoughts turned another way. "If you could give him up, you could give me up." That was really why I'd come. Not for Morgan's sake but for my own.

"I'd never give you up."

"How do you know?"

"Because I don't think you'd ever do anything like what Morey's done."

This was not comforting. It depended on circumstances. What good was loyalty that changed with circumstances? It was circumstances we needed loyalty as protection against.

"What was it you always said, when we got to fighting over who got what? Blood's thicker than money?"

"It's not thicker than this, thicker than—" He left it blank and leaned in close to me. I could smell the whiskey on his breath. "He said once that he'd like to put Arlene in her place once and for all. In a trash can. Because she was trash." A laugh escaped him against his will, a high shrill laugh like Burt Reynolds'. He raised his head and waited for my reaction.

"So?" She was, I thought. High-class trash.

"Do you know where they found her?"

I shook like a wet dog, just once, involuntarily. It was the kind of detail that makes you think it's true, that nobody could have made this up. "Are you sure?"

He nodded. "Gagged and bound and dumped in a garbage can." I heard him slurp up the last of the whiskey.

"There might be another explanation."

"I'd be glad to hear it." He poured himself another glass. "It makes me just sick to think he did it. But I don't know what else to think."

I asked the bartender for a glass and poured myself a little Chivas from his bottle. The smell of it reminded me of my ex-husband. Right then I wished I had a husband to take care of me. I wished for anything other than to be on my own, at large in the world with only one eye.

I heard someone punch in something on the jukebox. Then Hank Williams was singing. "There's a tear in my beer, 'cause I'm crying for you, dear. You've been on my lonely mind."

I took a big gulp and liked the burning it made. "When are you going home?"

"I don't know, honey. This is not something you can fix with a big sloppy kiss. Your mother isn't willing to listen. Your mother needs her illusions."

I thought of her sitting me on her lap and telling me, when I was five years old, "Sarah, I hate to be the one to bring the bad news, I'm very sorry, but there is no Santa Claus." And before the question even came up, she said, with the same hangdog look, "There is no God." Maybe she couldn't face that there was no goodness. Maybe her limit of loss was Santa Claus and God. I could understand that because I was coming to my limit.

"Are you sure? Are you really convinced, once and for all, that he did it?"

"It makes my heart sick. It makes every decent thing I ever stood for dirty. But I am," he said, taking another drink. "I'm ashamed to be in the same family with somebody who'd do that to a woman."

I thought of Jake, of mentally tying him up, of handcuffing him with his hands behind his back, taping his mouth shut, tightening the rope on his ankles, and I tried to measure the distance between that thought and what my brother was supposed to have done. Not far enough.

"I bet a lot of people heard Morey say that. He probably said it all the time, like he does when he has a good thought, says it over and over until you're sick of hearing it. Remember how he used to say, 'Whatever gets it for you'? Or, when he saw a good looking woman walking down the street: 'Looks like lunch to me'? That's probably what happened. Or maybe somebody else had the same idea. I've thought it myself—that Arlene was trash. It's likely really. You know what it says in the Bible. There's nothing new under the sun."

I remembered another line, "All is vanity," and for the first time I saw the meaning. Not, all is vain, futile. But all is *vanity*. Dancing in front of the mirror. Preening for the cosmos. I thought of putting on a black leotard and tights and dancing in front of my bureau mirror, standing up on a chair to get a full-length view (though you couldn't take very big steps in that position, no strenuous leaps). I thought I looked fine, very sophisticated with my red hair back in a bun, white lipstick to make my eyes look larger, eyebrows dark with eyebrow pencil borrowed from my mother's dresser, my eyelashes black with forbidden mascara that would be under my eyes by the time the dance was done.

"Well, isn't it even *possible?*" I said too loudly and everyone at the bar looked up. I hunched over my drink then and tried to look inconspicuous.

My father kept slowly sipping his Chivas, the shadows burning into his face, making him old. "It's possible," he said after a while. "But so is dying happy."

I looked at myself in the mirror behind the bar, in the distortions of silver and lead. You couldn't see that I had one eye. Both eyes were in shadow. I looked at my father, one in a long line of daytime drunks, the room too dark to give him any distinction except his full head of black hair. I didn't want Morey to be guilty, not for his own sake, but for mine. I didn't want to be the sister of a murderer, a humiliator of women. My mind was mixed up with sympathy and disgust and vindictiveness. I wanted Morey to pay for all the meanness he'd inflicted on my body and my life. I wanted to see him set free, to come driving up in his red Maserati. I wanted to hear him say, "It's like kissing your sister." I wanted our family to be what I had once thought it was.

Sɪɴᴇ ᴡᴀs ᴜᴘ ᴏɴ ᴀ sɪx-ꜰᴏᴏᴛ
ladder in the living room when I came home from high school that
day, putting masking tape over the cracks in the open brick wall, a
piece of tape between the gray mortared edge of every brick.

"What are you doing?"

"I'm tired of these walls," she said. "I've decided I'd like them
smooth. Smooth and white. I'm going to tape all the little cracks, and
then I'm going to plaster over it."

"Will it stay? Like that?" The tape, I noticed, was beginning to
curl at the edges.

She looked at me and smiled. "I don't know. We'll find out, won't
we?" Then she almost fell off the ladder and I went to catch her.

"Oops," she said. "No dancing on the ladder." Then she laughed
and started talking a mile a minute.

"Granddaddy Grimes wouldn't let me go dancing when I was
your age, he said it was just belly-rubbing, sex standing up, but one
night my friend Irene asked me to go with her because she was afraid
to go alone, Irene was two years older than I was, she was seventeen
and I was fifteen, but I was the more adventurous, I guess you could
say, and she was my best friend so I went even though I knew Granddaddy Grimes would take the razor strap to me if he ever found out.

I had never been to a dance before, I thought it was so"—she hesitates, looking for the right word—"I don't know, grown people standing at the edge of a huge dark room, their eyes alive in the dark, the music loud, an excitement in the air you could feel in your fingertips. I remember the name of the band on the bass drum, it was called the Heartbeats, and there were two black notes painted on a big red heart." She made the shape with her arms, took a deep breath and continued, taping the little cracks, talking fast. "When the first boy asked me to dance I was surprised. Me? I said, looking in back of me. He nodded and took my hand and led me out onto the floor, I remember he had sweaty palms, I'd never had dancing lessons before but I knew how to dance, it must be something you're born with, something in your genes, my heart was beating hard and I'd never been so happy, and when it was over I felt my shoulders relax, I could breathe, I felt at home, and then the next boy asked me to dance—he was taller than the first boy, and older, much better looking, dark hair, a Roman nose—he spun me around so fast I thought my heart would burst and I laughed out loud, and with the next boy I did the Charleston—you don't know what that is because that was before your time, before the time you were born." Standing on the ladder, she demonstrated, her arms straight at her sides, shaking her shoulders and breasts while she bent her knees and leaned toward me, put one foot out, started to fall. I caught her again and she laughed. "Like that. You're supposed to have on a tight black dress with fringe all over it so it shakes when you shake. Then came a slow dance and three boys came up to me at the same time, I looked up into their faces and chose the one who looked the most scared, and when I took his hand he smiled. By the time the night was over twenty-seven boys had asked me to dance. Twenty seven. I kept track. That's the first night I knew I was beautiful. I met your father at a dance like that one, two years later, at the Blue Note in Tracy, and by then I knew I was something, I knew I was hot stuff, but he wasn't impressed, he didn't even notice, he seemed to like dancing better than looking at me, and I'd never danced with a man with such ... authority, he danced like he owned the whole God damn floor." She looked straight at me, paused in her crack covering, a woman who knew what she wanted. "I'd have followed him anywhere." Then she cackled, there's no other word for it. "When the dance was over he guided me back to my place with his hand at the base of my spine, it gave me chills, I can tell you that, and he said thanks for the dance, but he didn't hang around making moon eyes, he danced with a lot of other girls that night, and it was the first time I was jealous. I knew it was against all the rules, I knew it wasn't done, and I remember the sinking feeling in my stomach and my heart beating hard as I walked across the room with everyone watching. I said, May I have this dance? and held out my hand. He looked surprised, he looked shocked, but he was also secretly pleased, he told me that later, and he took my hand and we danced and by the time the dance was done we were as good as married." She paused finally and looked down at me. "What do you think?" she said, her green eyes bright, admiring one whole wall of taped cracks.

She spent six days and six nights in the living room, taping, plastering, and painting, talking at high speed when any of us was there to listen, maybe when we weren't, talking as if she couldn't talk fast enough to get all the words out. And after she was through, the living room walls were white swirled plaster instead of open brick, and nothing fell down, not then; the white walls were still standing until last Thanksgiving. The next day she collapsed and went to bed for a month, and would not answer when I knocked on her bedroom door, her shades drawn, her phone in a dresser drawer, my father sleeping on the porch swing, corn flakes for supper.

This is a photograph of the impression his sleeping body left on the flowered cotton mattress with white piping along the edges. It was 1963, the year John F. Kennedy was shot, the year my father would no longer do his chicken laugh. He said it hurt his throat, but I suspected even then that the real explanation was different. A window in the mind can go suddenly dark. Then another, and another. Like those mile-high buildings on Wilshire Boulevard at quitting time. The heart staggers, in good weather, heading for home.

THIS SIDE OF PORTLAND, I STARTED
getting tired. My back hurt and my neck was stiff. Twelve hours
straight, stopping only for coffee and gas. I started looking for a cheap
motel. When I didn't find one, I decided to keep driving, though I
can't see very well at night.

On my tapedeck Willie Nelson was singing, "I'll be all right in a
little while, but you'll be permanently lonely." I sang along, thinking
of Jake. I realized with a shock that I hadn't thought of Jake in several
days. I felt unfaithful. I tried to remember his face after making love,
the soft way his eyes looked, and couldn't. I tried to think of one thing
he'd said to me that was memorable. I thought and thought. "I love
you but I don't love you enough." That's all that was left, some last
words, intended to wound. But they didn't work. They were no
longer anything with power over my life.

It's interesting the way a person dies in your imagination. You ne-
glect their memory for a few nights and pretty soon you can't remember where the mole was placed, the exact shape of their ears, whether
their knuckles were thick or their fingers long and slender like your
own. Things you'd think you would never forget. You lose a feature at
a time, and then it's the sound of their voice that goes. You realize,
when you're imagining a conversation with them—conversations that

are starting to bore you—that it's your voice you're using for the whole thing, not just the parts where you speak. It's all your show, not only the good lines you give yourself, but the lines you make them say: "I was wrong. I'm sorry. The biggest mistake I ever made was leaving you." When the voice goes they've lost any real hold on you. Then it's the lovemaking, that trick they had of touching you in a certain way, you can't quite feel it. Maybe you even forget what it was. They become just one of the boys, nothing to distinguish them from the long line of lovers you've had and think of fondly but can't quite tell apart, their images run together in your mind—this one's pale thighs, another's dark-haired chest, those lovely hands. When they've joined the collage you're almost free. The test is when you come upon one of their old letters and the parts about what they've suffered— their rough childhood, the father that smacked them, the mother that drank and told them lies—those parts make you think, You're almost forty years old, honey, *grow up.*

Sympathy is the last thing to go, and sometimes it never does— with my ex-husband, for instance. As long as there's sympathy, sexual attraction is still possible. Every time I see my ex-husband we go to bed. We'll be eighty, I bet, and still sleeping together. I used to worry about it, that it wasn't normal, but now I think, You take your family traditions where you can find them.

It started snowing hard just past Coeur d'Alene and I almost drove my car into the lake, right there where Interstate 90 does that tricky turn northeast, up into the mountains. I switched on my defroster and my windshield wipers. My heart was pounding and I was straining to see, sure I'd get the perspective wrong and think the right set of high-way reflectors was really the left, and drive off into oblivion. Then I remembered something Sunny told me—that if you try too hard to see at night, you can't. It's one of those things you have to let go of to get. I rolled my shoulders back, took a deep breath, and punched the button to rewind the tape. Playing the same tape over and over is soothing, like saying a prayer. I've done it many times driving through snow. Once in Flagstaff, Arizona, doing ten miles an hour on ice, I played a Sammi Smith tape over and over, watching car after car spin donuts and then skid off into the embankment. Seven tow-trucks passed me, dumping snow onto my windshield, but I didn't stop. There is the illusion that if you lived through "Help Me Make It Through the Night" once, you'll do it again. I say "illusion" because the next tow-truck had my name on it.

Tonight, though, there were no tow-trucks in sight and I turned on my brights to see which way the road went. There were at least six cars in front of me, and none of them seemed to be thinking better of it, of going on, a thought I took some comfort from. The light was suffused with diagonally falling snow and it made it harder to see, so I clicked my lights back on low. The whirring sound stopped and I pushed in the PLAY button. I watched the line of cars move slowly through the bitter night with what I knew to be a stupid faith—faith that where the wheel needed traction there wouldn't be ice. I didn't believe it, though I unclenched my hands a little after a while, and settled back into a tolerable state of terror. "I'll be all right in a little while," I sang, "but you'll be permanently lonely."

I pulled into the Crossbar Inn at 3:15 Thursday afternoon. I'd slept for a few hours early that morning, in a truckstop parking lot, just before sunrise.

I looked in the rearview mirror to see how he would see me. Then I got out my comb and lipstick. I combed my bangs in a dip down over my right eye and put on lipstick. Other than lipstick, Rich had always hated makeup. He said he wanted to see my real face, not some painted doll's face. I took a deep breath, put the shoulder strap of my purse over my shoulder, and got out of the car. I saw his black truck parked in front of room 126. I wondered if he was in there or in the bar. I tucked in my blouse and walked across the parking lot.

Just as I raised my hand to knock on the door he opened it. "I was watching for you," he said, picking me up off the ground. He gave me a big hug. "Let's see this gruesome eye." He turned my face up to his, pushed the bangs back off my forehead. "It doesn't look too bad to me."

I started to cry. It's what I needed to hear, from someone who mattered. That it was still me, even after great bad luck.

"Poor baby," he said, putting me down. "Did you have a hard drive?"

"Not too bad," I said. "I made pretty good time."

He touched the pocket of his jacket to make sure he had his key, then he pulled the door closed. I walked behind him along the rock path to the glass doors that led into the lobby of the motel. I liked watching him from the back. He has broad shoulders and a narrow waist, about six feet tall. What my grandmother called well-built.

When we got to the glass doors he opened the door for me and waited for me to walk through. Inside, there were huge wooden crossbars that covered one wall, a freestanding fireplace in the middle of the room, surrounded by a hearth, with easy chairs further back. The desk was a circular thing that cut from the door across a third of the room, like the place they hand out shoes at a bowling alley. Two women were standing behind it, dressed in Levis and boots, their hair ratted like it was still the sixties.

"I reserved a room for you," he said. "If you want. Whatever you want is fine with me."

I wasn't sure at first what he meant. Then I got it. I could have my own room if I wanted it. But then I wasn't sure if it was what he wanted. I turned around to look at him, but his back was to me. I could hear music coming from the bar. Clint Black. "I'm Leaving Here a Better Man." I gave the clerk my name, signed the registration form, and got my key. 277. Nowhere close to 126.

"All set?" he asked. "Let's go have a drink." From the way he was walking, it looked like he'd had one already.

We sat down at the bar. The low light was soothing after last night's snow. I noticed the bar had a split in it like the bar at the Albatross after the Loma Prieta earthquake. I rubbed my index finger along the edge of it.

"Earthquake?" I said to the bartender.

"What?"

"Was there an earthquake?" I gestured toward the split.

"No. Just a little difference of opinion."

I smiled. "Looks pretty big to me."

"What'll it be?" he said, not smiling back. Maybe he had been one of the differences. Or maybe he didn't want to find out how I'd lost my eye.

"Bud Light."

"No more Jose Cuervo?" Richard asked. "If you don't drink tequila, I don't even know you."

"No more Jose," I said. "I'm hoping to become moderate in my old age."

"Bud Light," he said to the bartender. "And I'll have another Molson."

I smiled at him. "I guess that makes two of us." He used to drink Chivas Regal, straight up. All night long.

"Gettin' old," he said. "The old man can't put it away like he used to."

I took a sip of beer with a huge relief. Not to be on the road, afraid of sliding off mountains, dying in winter. Not to have to go anywhere outside this lowlit bar. Just to be here, safe, with someone I'd known since I was seventeen.

"Here's to you," I said, lifting my beer bottle.

"Here's to us," he said, clanking his bottle against mine.

We drank for a while in silence, and I waited for my eye to adjust to the dark. With only one eye, when you can't see, the feeling is worse than with two. I don't know why. Maybe it's just fear. I'm afraid something bad's going to happen and I won't be able to see it coming.

"So," Richard said. "What've you been doing?"

"Looking for a job," I said. "I'm not sure what I want to do." Putting it that way made it sound like more of a choice, being unemployed.

"What happened to that job down in L.A.? How did that pan out?"

"It was okay," I said, "but after you've taken photographs of all the animals in the zoo, the job's over. There's nowhere else to go. I suggested photos of the zookeepers, for publicity purposes. They said no." I shrugged and took another sip of beer.

He nodded, like he was thinking hard how to get me another job. "What about that place you did typing? What was it called?"

"Ted's Typing Service," I said. "They don't want me anymore. Not with this." I touched my fingers to my right eye, where it used to be. "Said it would scare the customers. The customers," I snorted. "Drug addicts, derelicts, and wackos."

"We've always got Paris," he said, then raised his beer bottle. Paris was where we were supposed to go on our honeymoon. But we spent the money my grandmother gave us on ski equipment instead.

The bar was starting to fill up. Couples at the tables, single men at the bar. There was only one other single woman, about sixty, on the other side of Rich. Short gray hair and a good face, a face like Katharine Hepburn's. But still sixty. I hoped I didn't end up like that, alone at a bar at sixty. I hoped I'd quit drinking by then and be somebody's grandmother, something to keep me home at night.

"How's Sarah?" I asked, making my voice singsong. Sarah is his second wife. She has the same name I do, which is something I've always resented. If he had to get married again, why couldn't he at least marry somebody with her own name?

"She's hanging in there," he said, smiling. After a few minutes, he said, "She didn't want me to come here today."

"Did you tell her you were meeting me?"

"I told her."

"What'd she say?"

"She said, Don't go. I don't want you to go."

Right then I felt some sympathy for her. But it passed.

"I told her I was going, but I made her a promise."

I knew what the promise was. That explained the two rooms. Jesus, wasn't there anything in life you could count on staying the same? But I said, "I understand."

We ordered another round, and I punched up some songs on the jukebox, songs we both liked. Patsy Cline singing "I Fall to Pieces." Hank Williams singing "Your Cheatin' Heart." K. T. Oslin singing "Do Ya?" He'd sent me a tape of that last Christmas. "Do ya still get a thrill when you see me comin' up the hill, honey now do ya? Do you whisper my name just to bring a little comfort to ya?" Staring into the light of the jukebox made it hard to see, so I took it slow walking back across the room.

"You're still skinny," he said. "I always knew you'd be a skinny old woman."

I smiled. For him this was pretty close to a compliment.

He took my hand and ran his thumb and middle finger up and down along each of my fingers. "Skinny," he said and smiled. "When I used to imagine you old, that's how I imagined you."

He looked a lot like I'd imagined him too. He was losing a little hair on top, but he still looked like himself. He'd put on maybe ten pounds in twenty years, that was it. And his eyes were still blue. Women still turned to watch him walk across a room.

"You don't look too bad yourself," I said.

"I do okay," he said. "The gir—, I mean the *women* still like me. At least the old . . . ones." I knew he'd been going to say *girls* and *broads*. I knew he was trying hard not to piss me off.

"I bet they do."

We kept falling into silences. Like there was something he'd come to talk about but he was putting it off.

"What's on your mind?" I asked after a while.

"Your kid," he said and snorted. "That God damn kid of yours." He laughed.

"He's a good kid," I said. "You should count your blessings that you're not bailing him out of jail, or picking out his casket after an overdose. Most kids that age are on drugs."

"That would be an improvement," he said. "Maybe then he'd have a drink with me."

I said, "He doesn't *drink,* for Christ sake." Right then I remembered how unreasonable Rich was when the world didn't go the way he thought it should. I remembered why I'd left him.

"My own kid, and he wouldn't even have a God damn beer with the old man."

"Now that's a tragedy," I said. "I don't know how you're going to live with that."

He laughed. "Okay. Maybe I overreacted. But Jesus, Sarah, I

always thought he'd come back to see me someday. I imagined it. How he'd sit down at a bar with me, knock back a few, and tell me about his life. Who he loved. What he wanted to be when he grew up. But he doesn't tell me anything."

"That's not the way I heard it. I heard you made fun of everything he said. Like what you said when he told you he wanted to be a writer."

"What?"

"'Money talks, bullshit walks'?"

He laughed. "Maybe I shouldn't have said that. But Jesus, a writer. Is that something for a man to be? Is that why I sent him to college?"

"You didn't send him to college. He paid his own way. You didn't give him a dime after the first semester."

"He's ashamed of me," he said. "That's it. He doesn't think my life is worth shit. I just wanted him to see . . ."

"To see what?"

"To see how I spend my time. To show a little interest."

"That's all he wanted from you. For you to think what he did was important." I looked at him. "You're the *father*, for Christ sake."

"You're right." He looked sad for a moment. "Okay."

"I want you to call him, or write. I don't want you ruining this family." I started to cry, thinking of Morgan in jail, and Mom and Daddy splitting up.

"Hey," he said. "Don't do that. I'm sorry. Hey." He put his palm on my cheek and rubbed his thumb under my eye.

"Then you better do something to fix it. Call him. Write. For Christ sake."

"Okay," he said. "I'll write to him. But God damn it. A writer." He shook his head. "Like words could change anything."

"Leave him alone. Let him be what he wants. What does it matter to you? You're turning out just like your father."

He didn't talk for a while, but his eyes were moving, and I knew he was thinking. He said, "You're right. I never thought about that. The old bastard. He never could give me any credit. I'm turning into the old fart himself. Old Fart, Junior."

"Just write to him."

"I will," he said and nodded like he meant it. "For you."

I got up to go to the bathroom. All that beer. "Which way?" I asked.

He pointed. But he kept looking at me.

"What?"

He shook his head. "Skinny," he said and smiled.

When I got back to the bar he was talking to the old woman on the other side of him. Her eyes were lit up like it was Christmas.

I sat down, and he introduced her to me. "Edna," he said, "I'd like you to meet my wife, Sarah. I mean my *ex*-wife."

"Pleased to meet you," Edna said. "Your husband here was just telling me about Missoula. I'm new to the area."

"*Are* you? Well, I hope you like it here." I kept the enthusiasm in my voice to a minimum, and I didn't ask where she was from. I wanted to get back to our conversation, minus the old woman. I wanted to get down to some serious talk about the good old days.

"He said it was the worst smog outside of L.A. On account of it being in the valley and all."

"Really," I said. "I'll be darned."

Rich caught the bartender's eye and gestured to our two empty beer bottles and to the old woman's glass. "Whatever she's having," he said.

"Why thank you," she said and turned on the white teeth.

"Nobody's bought me a drink in quite some time."

"Let's go sit at a table," I said. "I'm getting a little hungry. Maybe we could order some potato skins or some nachos."

"We can get those right here at the bar," Rich said, handing me the plastic-covered menu. "Anything your little heart desires."

That was one of the things he used to say. Anything your little heart desires. When he took me out to dinner. When we were in bed. I looked at him to see if he was thinking what I thought he was thinking, but no look of enlightenment came over his face. Maybe he'd kept on saying it over the years until it had lost its original meaning. That was possible, I guess.

I studied the menu for a few minutes. "I'll have the mushroom burger," I said. "Medium rare. Hold the onions."

"Are you hungry, Edna?" he asked. "Would you care to join us?"

She giggled. A sixty-year-old woman, giggling. "No, but I thank you very much for the invitation." She squeezed his arm. It didn't matter what age they were, sixteen or sixty, he knew how to get his arm squeezed.

He turned back to me, and I jerked my head to indicate the old woman.

"What?"

I leaned toward him and whispered, "Knock off the charm, George, unless you prefer her company to mine." George was his middle name, which I used when I wanted his full attention.

"I was just being polite," he said.

"Saying hello is polite. Tipping your hat is polite."

"Okay," he said. "I won't say another word." He turned to her then. "Excuse me, ma'am, but my wife doesn't like me talking to such a good-looking woman. She gets jealous. You understand."

The old woman giggled again. "Perfectly," she said. "I understand perfectly." She took her glass and moved over a little, toward the end of the bar.

He turned back to me. "Are you happy now? I hope you're happy."

I nodded my head. "I'm happy."

"Good." He looked at me carefully. "I'd forgotten what you were like. I'd forgotten how you . . ."

"What?"

"Nothing," he said. "This is supposed to be a reunion. This is supposed to be a good time. Let's not spoil it."

The bartender set our beers down in front of us. "I'll drink to that," I said.

We sat there at that bar for two or three more hours. We saw it get dark through the stained glass window behind the bartender's head. Rich was starting to slur his words, and the last time I went to the restroom I was bouncing off walls like a pinball.

The bartender set two more beers down in front of us. "From the lady at the end of the bar," he said.

Rich said, "Thank you." He didn't say it really, just mouthed the words to the old woman and pointed at the beer. To me he said, "What do you say we call it a night?"

"Are you tired?"

"I've had enough to drink, I can say that much."

I took his arm and pulled him up off the barstool. We left a tip and started to walk out.

"Have a nice night," Edna called out to us.

Rich went back and bent down to her, whispered something in her ear. What'd she do? She giggled.

"What'd you say?" I asked when he came back.

"That's between me and Edna," he said.

I shook my head, but I was in too good a mood to say anything more. I took his arm and we walked across the lobby, out into the cold night. The moon was full, and the snow looked like foam from a spilled beer, piled waist-high at the edge of the parking lot.

"Which way's my room?" I said, fumbling for the key in my purse.

"Right here," Rich said, patting his chest twice with his open palm.

I considered reminding him of his promise. Then something inside me said, Yield to temptation. It may not pass your way again.

He got out his key and tried to fit it in the lock. He said, "This is the first test."

I said, "What's the second?"

He laughed. We both laughed.

He shut the door and took off his hat. "Can you help me with these boots?" he said, sitting on the edge of the bed. I held the heel with both hands against my stomach while he pulled his foot out. Then the other one.

"Still can't get undressed by yourself," I said.

"Come here," he said. He pulled me down on the bed beside him and I slipped off my shoes, then peeled off my socks. He kissed me, just lightly. "Would you like a little help with those buttons?" He started unbuttoning my blouse. When they were all undone he said, "Stand up." I was surprised but I did as he asked. "Now take off the blouse. Slowly," he said. "And the rest. I want to watch."

The only light in the room was coming from outside, through the split in the curtains. You could barely see. He got up and turned on the bathroom light, which was around the corner, shut the door half-way, so the light cut the room in half diagonally, then came back and lay down on the bed.

I slipped the blouse off my shoulders, and then noticed I wasn't breathing. I took a deep breath. This was someone I knew, someone

I'd made love to for thirteen years. Why was I scared? I let the blouse drop to the floor. I stood there in my black lace bra and Levis, not knowing what to do next.

He got up and came around behind me, unhooked the bra, then he slipped his hands up under the cups, over my breasts. "I don't want you to stop," he said. "I just wanted to touch you. I couldn't wait." He kissed my neck and then went back to the bed.

I was maybe three feet away from him. I hooked my thumbs under the straps of the bra and shrugged it off. I stood there in front of him, not making a move. Then I unbuttoned the top button of my Levis. I imagined I heard "The Stripper" playing somewhere far off, and I laughed.

"What's so funny?" he asked.

"Nothing," I said, but laughing helped, I wasn't scared anymore. I unbuttoned the rest of the buttons on my Levis. I looked right at him. Then I inched them down my thighs, first one side, then the other. The Levis were tight and to do it gracefully took quite a while. Finally I stepped out. Now all I had on were black bikinis.

"Just stand there," he said. "I wanted to remember you, what you looked like." I could hear him breathing.

I put my arms out to my sides and turned around, like I was in a fashion show. There was a heaviness in the room, something brooding, and out of nerves I laughed again. "The latest fashion," I said, "in ladies' apparel."

"Every night I go over it," he said. "Your mouth. Your breasts. But I was starting to forget. I don't want to forget. That's the real reason I asked you to come."

I felt some hardness that had been forming inside me loosen, break free. I went over to the bed. "I'm right here," I said. "Any time you want to see me, I'm right here."

He reached out and pulled me down to the bed. I could feel the rough material of his Levis against my bare skin, the cold metal grips at my hipbones.

"You feel the same," he said, and I thought it was strange because to me he felt brand new and like someone I'd always known. Both.

"I never stopped wanting you," he said. I said, "Me too," and wondered if it could be true. Could you leave someone you'd never stopped wanting? He slipped the tip of one finger into my mouth and it seemed like an answer.

I said, "I love you," and he said, "I know," which is what he always said on the phone when we were ready to hang up, so nobody in the room on his end would know what he meant. I remembered that when my first book of photographs came out, *California Home,* he called up where I worked and left me a message. Ted handed me the pink slip when I came back from lunch. It said, *I know.*

"Do you think about me sometimes?" I asked. "When you can't sleep?" Rich didn't sleep much at night either. He used to say I'd be sorry if I ever left him, because who else would stay up half the night and keep me company?

"I have a confession to make." He moved his hand slowly over the ruined eye as if to heal it. "Every fantasy I ever had—you were in it," he said, and the way he looked at me I could tell that he didn't really see the eye, that it wasn't part of his picture of me, and that nothing could make him see me other than I'd been at seventeen, as close as I would ever come to pretty. I could feel my heart beating in my stomach as I moved against him.

He held me cradled in his arms, one arm around my shoulders, one arm under my knees, and for some reason I thought of being lifted in the dark, in the midst of dreaming, with great consideration, carried heavy with sleep from the car up the stairs to my bed when I was a child. Taken care of. And when he pulled me on top of him I closed my eyes, felt my body give up its vigil, felt relieved of the weight of myself for the first time since Jake left.

"Sex after long deprivation," I said, "it's the closest I've come to religion."

He laughed. "I want you to tell me what you want," he said, "it's been so long, tell me, anything your little heart desires."

My heart was beating too hard and I said, to slow it down, "Will you stand out on the balcony naked and whistle 'Dixie'?"

He laughed again. "Anything except that." Then he put his hands in my hair and pulled my face close to his, so close that even in the dark I could see his eyes. "Anything." And I believed it was true, that no desire was outcast, every wayward longing would be welcomed in.

Afterwards we talked easily, as if there hadn't been years in between. We talked about the places we'd lived. Remember Tucson? Remember Juneau? Remember Santa Monica? Then it got more specific. Remember that orange plastic furniture we had in our first apartment? The formica end table with rusted legs? Remember how you cried when Sunny was born?

"Remember how *you* cried on our six-month anniversary? You were eight months pregnant and we went out to a fancy place we couldn't afford, out on the pier, what was it called?"

"The Cheerio," I said.

"Right. The Cheerio. You ordered filet mignon and when it came it was burnt on the outside and raw in the middle. Your face puckered up, and you started to cry, big old tears dripping down your cheeks. And the waiter said, 'Please, miss, *please* don't cry,' and he picked up your steak knife, closed his eyes, and aimed it at his heart."

I laughed. "It was burnt *and* raw, for Christ sake." I elbowed him in the ribs. "Remember when we lived in North Sacramento? There was that waitress who worked at Sam's Hofbrau. The one with the beehive hairdo. Every time she saw you she almost had an orgasm."

"I don't remember," he said.

"She had rhinestone glasses, pointed at the corners." I made the points with my thumbs and forefingers.

"Oh yeah," he said. "Now I remember. She always drew a happy face on the back of the check and signed it, *Thanks! Starletta.*"

"What about her?" I asked.

"What about her what?"

"Did Starletta have anything to thank you for?"

"I never touched her," he said. "I swear." He held up his hand like a man taking an oath.

"What about that woman in Santa Monica?" I asked. "She had long black hair, clear down to here. She was the sister of our next-door neighbor. Leslie something. Whenever she saw you she turned beet red. What about her?"

"Okay," he said. "I confess. I made love to her in the pool house."

When he said that my mind started racing, from California to Texas to Arizona to Alaska. This was my chance, my chance to know everything.

"What about that woman in Galveston? The one whose husband turned out to be gay, the one who worked for NASA?"

"Who?"

"You remember. She had four sons, and a grand piano in her apartment living room. She always looked at you like she was hungry. What was her name?"

"Helen," he said.

"You slept with her, didn't you?"

"I wouldn't call it sleeping." He had his arm under my shoulders and he pulled me in close to him.

"I knew it." I waited a minute to see how it made me feel, but nothing cracked, nothing hurt. "At least you're honest," I said. Then I laughed. "I *knew* it."

"What about that Indian woman who had the hots for you? I saw her at every rodeo, sitting on the fence in her tight jeans and white blouse, and I knew she could guess what event you did best in. Did you sleep with her?"

"No. That's one I missed."

"God, she was beautiful. I thought you were in love with her. I could have understood it if you were." I ran my hand along his thigh.

"Okay," he said. "I was in love with her. But only a little. Nothing like I was with you." He leaned over and kissed me. It was quiet for a few minutes and I was smiling in the dark. Then he touched my forearm. "What about you? Were you so pure all those years?"

"I have always been faithful." The way I said it, "The Star-spangled Banner" could've been playing in the background.

"Come on," he said. "You're talking to me now. I told you what you wanted to know. Now it's your turn."

I thought of that summer in Arizona, of the four-by-six-foot collage of photographs that hung in my closet, titled *The Summer of Men:* this one's pale thighs, another's dark-haired chest, those lovely hands. How many were there? Twenty? Thirty? I didn't understand it but I did it, and part of me liked it. As abruptly as the desire came on the end of that April, it stopped. September first. I still remember the day. I woke up calm, the way you feel when you've made an important decision. I was no longer . . . possessed. I had never told anyone. I was ashamed. But proud in a perverse way. I *will* do what I want! I *will* do what I want! The Summer of Men was the only time during our marriage that I had been unfaithful to my husband. The degree of it made "unfaithful" seem the wrong word to choose. Like saying you'd hurt someone you'd killed and stuffed into a garbage can.

"Come on," he said. "It's just me here."

I was drunk and I felt at home and in the spirit of reciprocity I told him the truth. Some of it anyway. "The man in Phoenix," I said. "He was the only one." I was still smiling.

The air in the room changed. I felt the hairs rise on the back of my neck before he even said anything.

He yanked his arm out from under me. "Jesus Christ, Sarah, I was only kidding. I never touched any of those women."

I wasn't drunk anymore. My eye was wide open.

"And you made me feel guilty for taking a swing at you when I caught you in his truck."

"We hadn't done anything then."

"When?" he said. "How many times?"

"Jesus Christ, Richard, it was ten years ago."

"Where?" he said. "Was it in his camper? Did you fuck in the back of his camper?"

"No," I said. "It wasn't there."

"It wasn't in my house, was it? Not in our bed. Please tell me it wasn't in our bed."

"No, it wasn't," I said. "I don't want to talk about it. This is ridiculous." My heart was beating hard. "It was ten years ago. This is ridiculous."

"My own wife," he said. "Son of a bitch. I don't know how you could do that to me." I could feel him staring at me in the dark.

"There were so many women after you all the time, I didn't think you'd notice."

"I never touched any of them," he said. "I looked, sure, I *looked*. But that's all."

"I'm sorry," I said. "I'm really sorry."

"Where did you do it?" he asked again. "How many times?"

"It was at his place in Scottsdale," I said. "And it only happened twice." *Happened.* That was a good word to use.

"The son of a bitch," he said. "I should have wiped that smug look off his face."

I touched his arm and he pulled it away. "Jesus Christ," he said. "My own wife."

He didn't say anything for a long time. "Talk to me," I said. "Don't let me lay here feeling bad all alone."

"I'm just thinking about the past. How it explains a lot," he said. "Like how my son looks at me."

"He didn't know," I said. "I never told him. Why would I do that?"

"He looks at me just like he'd look at me if he knew."

"Let's go to sleep," I said miserably. "We're both drunk. Let's talk about it in the morning." I got up and turned off the bathroom light, came back and got carefully into bed. I wanted to touch him but I didn't think I had the right.

"Nothing is what I thought," he said. "Nothing. Our whole life."

We didn't talk about it in the morning. He didn't bring it up and I didn't know how. We had breakfast at the inn restaurant. We made smalltalk while we waited for the food to come. Scrambled eggs, English muffins, hash browns. The sun shone on the snow outside the window, and it made his eyes look bluer than usual. I watched the careful way he ate, the way he held his fork, his hands. I had never loved him more than I loved him that morning when I thought I had ruined our past.

After breakfast he said he had to go check out the substation. He asked if I wanted to ride along, to keep him company. He didn't act like he was mad, but his movements were slow, elegiac. Or maybe they only seemed that way because I thought I might never be with him again.

I sat close to him in the truck, with my left hand on his thigh, the way we used to ride when we were married. We drove west for many miles on Interstate 90. You could see a long ways, and there were no other cars on the highway. It was way too quiet, the kind of quiet that has a pulse. There was a Willie Nelson tape in the tape-deck and I pushed it in, but the sound of his voice made me cry, so I turned it off.

I said, "Are you all right?" The sky was blue against the snow and I knew I would remember how it looked that day, that blue sky against white snow on an empty highway would bring it back.

He said, "I'll live."

There was a smokestack in the distance, with puffs of smoke coming out of it at regular intervals, and I thought of somebody sending signals.

"Can you forgive me?"

"I'm going to have to think about it," he said. "Right now, I can't really get my mind around it."

I looked at his profile and nodded. "Will you tell me? If you ever forgive me?"

He said, "I will."

When we got back to the parking lot at the inn I opened the door on my side of the truck, jumped down. He walked with me to my car. I unlocked my door, set my suitcase inside. Before I got in he hugged me hard and I felt the cold smooth material of his down jacket against my cheek, and it filled me with sorrow, this man who was dear to me above all others and now would be . . . what? I didn't know. Lost, anyway. And it was worse knowing it was what I'd done myself, something I'd had control of, that could have been different, like losing my eye.

I said, "I love you," and he said, "I know," and I knew the meaning had changed.

I played the music loud driving back, and the sun on the bright glass blinded me, and the curving road through the mountains made my stomach sick and my heart rise and sink. I cried all the way, hard body-shaking sobs. Until it got dark. Then I couldn't afford to cry any longer. High up in the mountains, where Montana and Idaho meet, it started to snow, and I turned the windshield wipers on. Every few miles I saw a sign that warned of ice you couldn't see. Black ice. I knew I should stop for the night in Coeur d'Alene, but I wanted to get home, find somewhere to quietly sit and assess the damage. An eighteen-wheeler passed me on a downhill grade, spewing snow onto my windshield, and for several minutes I couldn't see. I turned the windshield wipers on high, shifted down, and called him a son of a bitch. "Our Father which art in Heaven—*Our Father-Mother-God, all-harmonious*—hallowed be Thy name—*Adorable One.* Thy kingdom come. *Thy kingdom is come; Thou art everpresent.*" I didn't believe a word of it, but it made me picture my grandmother Blight and the deep calm blue of her eyes, and the familiar sound of her words said out loud soothed me. "Thy will be done, in earth, as it is in heaven. *Enable us to know—as in heaven, so on earth—God is omnipotent, supreme.*" When I went around the truck driver going up, he dimmed his lights to let me know it was safe to pass, and I put my hand up to thank him, and he dimmed his lights again. "Give us this day our daily bread—*give us grace for today; feed the famished affections.*" I'd never really heard the words before. Famished affections. I pictured Edna sitting alone at the bar. "And forgive us our debts, as we forgive our debtors. *And Love is reflected in love.*" Right then I saw a jackknifed motorcycle, nose down in the snowbank a foot below the edge of the road, its rear wheel slightly spinning, the driver nowhere in sight. I felt like that's what had been done to my life. Then I saw Rich's face, and saw what I'd done to his life, and I knew I wasn't sorry for him alone but for ruining his memory of me. "And lead us not into temptation, but deliver us from evil, *and God leadeth us not into temptation, but delivereth us from sin, disease, and death.*" The snow began to blow harder, from another direction, and all I could see was the snow and the black night and the windshield wipers scraping over the iced-up glass. It let up a little on the next curve south, and I could see that there were six or seven cars ahead of me on the road, but I decided to stay where I was, that doing twenty miles an hour in such weather was good enough. The eighteen-wheeler passed me again on the next downhill grade, and his tires sprayed a steady stream of snow onto my windshield and covered up the glass. "For Thine is the kingdom. And the power." This time I didn't try to see. A caravan of cars moved slowly through the snow-blowing night as if by faith in the human enterprise. Faith that where the wheel needed traction there wouldn't be ice. Faith the eye would find the next reflector, that the road would go on in the dark. "Amen."

part two

REASONABLE GRIEF

❧

"Bipolar affective disorder,
with secondary alcoholism, complicated by G-A-D," she said, reading
from her clipboard as if the diagnosis had come from somewhere else.

"I only drink when I'm anxious or depressed," I said in my defense. "What's G-A-D?"

"Generalized Anxiety Disorder."

"Oh," I said, my confidence in freefall. "And bipolar whadaya-
callit?"

"Bipolar affective disorder. Another name for manic depression."

"Another name for all messed up."

She smiled her cryptic smile and went on with her little speech
about side-effects, blood tests, windows of something-or-other.

At first, I'll admit, I was elated. Everything explained. Every delu-
sion of grandeur, fall from grace, every ungrounded terror or night
sweat, every protestation of love, however quickly retracted, every
excess of sex or self pity—all vindicated. My mother always said I
had only two gears: overdrive and reverse. I could see this now as
metaphor. If the thermometer is busted, what looks like snow may not
be cold.

After the elation, of course, came depression; after the grand explanation, grave doubt. Can we be certain then of any weather? It is

prudent never to wholly trust what has once deceived us. But what if
what has deceived us is ourselves?

When I looked up she was explaining the benefits of drug ther-
apy. Lithium. Prozac. Howitzers for the brain.

She held out two prescriptions, which I left dangling from her
thumb and forefinger. Now that I knew I was really sick and not just
seeing things clearly, I wasn't sure I wanted the drugs. I was afraid of
becoming one of those people who think they're happy mainly because they don't have the concentration to sustain a negative thought.
Any thought.

"I don't want to end up a zombie," I said.

"This medication won't make you a zombie. It'll enable you to
sleep, to concentrate, give you more energy, less anxiety. Control your
mood swings."

"I'm used to my mood swings. I *like* my mood swings. Without
my mood swings I don't know *who* I . . ."

"It's up to you, of course."

I said I'd think about it, and she handed me a book with a woman
on the cover who looked a lot like me—the left side of her face with
the one good eye, wide open, the other side of her face in shadow, the
eye blacked out. *Manic Depression and the Meaning of Life.* "See if you
recognize yourself in any of this," she said.

*Manic depressives seem to have unlimited energy, talk nonstop, and
need very little sleep,* I read as I walked toward the elevator.

I thought of my mother taping all the little cracks in the living
room walls, talking a hundred miles a minute, hanging the wash in the
middle of the night, naked.

I pushed the DOWN button.

Depression, suicide, and alcoholism are common in such family trees.

I thought of Grandfather Blight and the minus-seven circled in red. I thought of my great grandmother, Victoria, dancing at the edge of the abyss. I thought of my father Ray.

The more I read the more I recognized, and I began to think of other scenes of family life in a new perspective.

I saw Mama taking me shopping for school clothes and buying eleven pairs of shoes all the same style but in different colors, eleven identical blouses and eleven skirts, eleven pairs of underpants with the day of the week written in cursive on the left hip, stopping with pink Wednesday in the second set. "Because," she said, "eleven is our lucky number."

They often cannot control their impulses, spending more money than they have, and they may experience hypersexuality or insatiable sexual desire.

I saw my brother driving up in a red Maserati with a present for Arlene--a two-carat diamond ring in a solitaire setting--when all he had in the bank was a few hundred dollars. His favorite saying that year was, "If you can't drive it, eat it, wear it, or make love to it, I don't want it."

I saw the collage of photographs in my closet titled *The Summer of Men*.

Then there was the day Uncle Ad flew from Stockton Field to Brennan's in New Orleans for Bananas Foster. He took me and Morgan with him because we were around when the whim came to him in the form of a moral imperative: vanilla ice cream with long slices of banana over the top, brown sugar and butter for the sauce, rum for the fire. Served in a silver dish, made right in front of us. It was the best thing I ever tasted. There were white table cloths. The waiters all spoke French, and they treated us as if we were fragile and would-break. There was a hush in the room, I remember that too. A quiet that only money can accomplish.

When we were through, Uncle Addison said, "Had enough?" I looked at him for a minute to see if he really wanted the truth, then shook my head. "Encore!" Uncle Addison said to the waiter, gesturing to all three silver dishes.

"Encore!" Morgan and I yelled, giddy with pleasure and high on sugar. Everyone in the room turned to look at us.

"I'd like you to meet my nephew and my niece," Uncle Addison said, "the king and queen of South Manteca." He stood up, then bowed at the waist, showed Morgan how to bow while I curtsied like Shirley Temple.

When we got home, Aunt Martha was screaming and threatening to call the little men in white coats.

"I *tol-l-ld* you to keep taking your medication," she said. "But *no-o-o*. You thought you were *well-l-l.*" Her voice rose and fell like an ambulance siren. "I warned you. Don't say I didn't warn you. And now look what you've done. How will we ever pay for it? We're still paying off that little trip to Las Vegas you took in 1953." She started to wail and pull at her hair. Of the two, I thought she was the more in need of medication.

"When we're dead, Martha, who'll care?" Uncle Addison said. "Why not live a little while we're here?"

Was Uncle Ad a manic depressive?

Maybe manic depression ran in families, like alcoholism and agoraphobia and a tendency toward cat-killing. Maybe we all had a defective gene that could take different forms, start different cracks moving in different directions. I saw my mother swaying at the top of the ladder, admiring her work, all the little taped cracks in all the brick walls—a maniac's labyrinth with no way out. Your family. People you think are normal because they're the people you know best, your only example of what normal is. But they're nuts and you're nuts too and how would you ever discover it?

The elevator doors opened and closed, but I didn't get in. Instead I suffered vertigo, a sensation of falling, I couldn't breathe, I felt like someone was choking me, and then, as if from far off, I heard a low yowling sound like a cat in heat, a sound that sang of desperation, of chaos, a sound you wouldn't want to hear coming from your own mouth.

THE LITTLE GIRL IS PICKING
daisies and throwing them into the water, disturbing the transparent
surface of the pond. She has fine red hair and blue eyes. Through a
knothole in a tall gray wooden fence someone is watching. We see a
thought cross his face. Then Frankenstein's monster throws the little
girl into the pond. There are bubbles. She doesn't come up.

That's when Morgan threw the wet washcloth on the back of my
neck, and I screamed and screamed and could not be comforted.

Angela said, trying to soothe me, "He couldn't help it. He didn't
make himself."

"They took me to a place I did not want to go," my grandmother said, grabbing at my hand. Her eyes darted back and forth and she kept her voice low. "They, those men, they took me out into the country, a long way from here. I was so afraid, I didn't know how I would get back, not having any transportation, you know. They took me to a basement and left me a good long time. It seemed like four hours but it is hard to judge these things. I was so cold, I almost cried out of self-pity." I held her hand and petted it. "A man came in. He was very arrogant—you know how they are sometimes—and he tells me what to do in a ..." Her voice faded away and I didn't catch what she said. "He said he was going to look me over. He unzipped my gown and did ... all manner of things." The color rose in her cheeks. "I just closed my eyes and pretended I was somewhere else. Back in Colfax living the life of Riley." She smiled and then abruptly frowned. "I don't understand, I'm so confused. The nice Practitioner came. She prayed for me but there is so much interference with thought here. It's amusin' but confusin'." She smiled again. Then she looked at me and waited to make sure I was looking back. "They stuck needles in my hip"—here she lifted up the blankets to show me where and there were bandages on the tissue-thin skin visible at the edge of her twisted nightgown—

"and my pink shawl is missing," she said, pointing at her closet in the corner. "And they've taken Ellen." Here she pointed up at the wall, where the picture of my mother had been. "Well?" she said, as if I should get on it right away, do something to restore order and sanity to the universe.

"What do you want me to do, Grandmother?"

"They took me to a place I did not want to go," she said again, her lips a straight line, her eyes stopped down, as if what I should do next were self-evident.

"I'll be right back," I said, and went to talk to the nurse behind the reception desk. It was Miss Franklin, the one with the sincere and cheerful smile. She looked up at me.

"I see you've brought your camera with you again today, Miss Blight. Taking snapshots of Grandma, are we?"

"My grandmother," I said very precisely, "claims she was taken somewhere against her will."

"Excuse me?"

I repeated myself.

"Oh, I don't think she's been anywhere further than the Bingo room," she said, smiling. "I think that's part of, uh, her, um . . ."

"*Disease?* She doesn't believe in disease. That's the point. She said they took her to what sounded a lot like a hospital. Gave her shots. How did she get the bandage on her hip if it isn't true? She's never been to a doctor in her *life!*" On *life* my voice went shrill and it gave me a slight headache.

"I'll certainly try to find out, Miss Blight. Let me check with her doctor of record and I'll get right back to you."

"He's the one who promised *not* to put her in a hospital. That's why we *chose* him." I wanted instant results, instant capitulation. "My grandmother is a Christian Scientist," I said moving my lips as if articulating for the deaf. "Do you understand what that means? Her greatest fear in life was ending up in a hospital. She said, just now, to me, in her room, 'They took me to a place I did not want to go.' Where else could that be?" I knew I was repeating myself, trying for a better answer the next time out.

"I'll find out right away, Miss Blight," said the imperturbable Miss Franklin, experienced in dealing with guilty relatives who used their outrage to convince themselves of their unselfish devotion to the welfare of demented grandmothers, panic-stricken mothers, besotted fathers, lost sons. "I'll call you or have someone call you tonight. Earlier, if possible." She smiled and nodded her kindergarten encouragement at me.

"All right," I said as if it were a threat and something good had better be forthcoming pretty damn fast.

I went back down the hall toward my grandmother's room, sullen at heart. Now the pastel prints of turquoise cactus and sand-colored haciendas in a pink sky seemed as phony as the place they were meant to enliven, as pointless as the television she endlessly watched, unable to discern the meaning of the stories within stories, lust- and tear-filled soap operas punctuated by women cheerfully scrubbing floors and hawking shampoo or aspirin or feminine hygiene products, the news all mixed up with fantasy and violence and Entertainment Tonight. Playing Bingo for an intellectual change of pace. Wasn't that dreaming enough? The only thing in the world she had requested before her mind was gone was not to be taken to a hospital, not to be handed over to the men in white coats, not to be treated like a piece of meat when she was a soul.

I came into the room and she looked directly at me for the first time in months and said, "Sarah," and although it may have been my imagination, I thought her voice held grief.

I began, as if the prayer were my own. "There is no life, Truth, intelligence, nor substance in matter. All is infinite Mind and Its infinite manifestation." I patted her hand, pulled the blanket up to her chest, smoothed the edge of the sheet over it, and from somewhere deep inside where everything important was kept, free from sin, disease, and death, it came out.

"Spirit is the real and eternal," she said, "matter is the unreal and temporal. Spirit is God, and man is His image and likeness. Therefore man is not material; he is spiritual."

She smiled at me and I smiled back, conspirators in a dead language.

I held her hand and tried to perform what had become by then a ritual, to think of some good memory, to bring her spirit back, so that the last few months of her life would not eclipse the past. But I could think of no good memory.

"It's a great life if you don't weaken," she said and laughed, shook her head in fond disgust at the world's absurdities, us among them. That's when I clicked the shutter and caught her exact face. And I thought, This is enough. Now. What she is now.

A man in a wheelchair was blocking the front door, trying to open it, banging it against the metal frame of his chair over and over. There was no way for him to get close enough to the door to open it without the wheelchair being in the way. He looked up at me and grabbed my hand, a look of terror and pleading.

"Can I get out of here on your ticket?"

"We are made in God's image and likeness," I told him, setting his hand back in his lap, repeating phrases from my grandmother's life. "Sin, disease, and death are illusions, errors of human belief and mortal sense. Evil does not exist. God is Life, Truth, and Love." I patted his mottled hand.

"Please," he said, but I didn't look him in the eye or in any way respond as if I'd heard. I moved around him like somebody traversing a familiar room in her sleep, like he was furniture.

"We are made in God's image and likeness," I repeated as I unlocked the car door, got in, and then, looking into my rearview mirror, began to laugh.

I turned up the volume on the tape deck until I could no longer think. It was an old tape of Janis Joplin singing "Get It While You Can." I thought of Rich and of Jake and of all the other men I had loved and betrayed or who had loved and betrayed me, and I thought then that we were not made in any god's image and likeness but were more like falling objects, not masters of our fate or captains of our soul but accidents looking for a place to happen.

"Can I get out of here on your ticket?" I whispered over the screaming of the music.

IN THE PICTURE HE IS SIX OR seven. He's standing at the edge of a swimming pool in turquoise swimming trunks a size too big, squinting into the sun. His Marine sergeant father has his huge hand wrapped around Jake's scrawny upper arm, getting ready to toss him in, saying, "Sink or swim. That's life, Jakey boy." He didn't sink but he didn't swim either. He gulped down water and flailed. When he came up for air his face was blue and he no longer trusted anyone. He was fond of quoting Stevie Smith: "I was much further out than you thought, and not waving but drowning." Seeing him like that, just before it happened, fragile, not knowing his fate, made me feel something for him I'd never felt before. I thought for a moment that I knew what it was like to be him, to have that father.

I turned out the light, got into bed. But I immediately saw his face, the same blue eyes, the perfect white teeth—only this time he was twenty-nine, sitting on the barstool at the Sea Horse, all unknowing.

I turned on the light, got out of bed. I wanted to see that picture again. I stared at it hard, trying to see the boy in the man. I mentally transposed the picture in my hand onto the picture in my mind. I wondered where Jake was, if he was all right.

I picked up the telephone and dialed, without stopping to think.

He answered on the second ring. It didn't seem possible, him right there within easy reach, saying, "Hello? Who is this? Why don't you say something? Who *is* this?" Punching the button over and over, smacking at the receiver.

"It's me."

Silence.

"Sarah," I said.

"I know your voice." His voice was not sarcastic, accusing; it was unexpectedly soft.

"I just wanted . . ." What did I want? Why did I call? I stood there in my long T-shirt, legs shivering, and tried to think. The tree branches outside the window wavered and hit against the glass. "I just wanted to talk to you," I said and gripped the phone hard against my ear.

"I know."

I know? Meaning what? That he knew I had wanted to talk to him? That he knew because he'd wanted to talk to me?

"Jake." This had some authority in it.

"What, baby?"

"I don't understand. I don't understand what's happened. I would like to talk about it."

"I can't."

"Can't?"

"Can't. Won't. What's the difference?"

"The difference is whether I hate you or not."

He laughed, a surprised giggle that he choked off with a cough. "Sorry," he said, his voice low and grave. I could hear him picking his teeth with the silver dental instrument. He did it when he was nervous.

"I want to understand what's happened."

Silence.

"Well, I guess I'll go," I said, as if he had called me and I was getting impatient. I didn't want to go. I wanted him to say something that would make it possible for me to stay on the line, for us to keep talking.

"Jake?" I hugged my arms around myself and looked out at the dark, the edges of the glittering leaves outlined against the moon, and wondered what would become of me if I lost my other eye, who would lead me from room to room, whether there were shadows in the dark or was it all pitch black, like being a bat in a closet?

He whispered, "I don't know what to say." Then he waited, and I leaned toward the silence. Finally, he spoke. "I want to ask if you're all right."

"No, I'm not all right. I have a *hole* in my face. I'm an honest-to-God walking-talking freak. I don't know if I'll ever be all right again."

I could hear his sharp intake of breath. This is breaking all the rules, I thought, this unattractive shrillness, this unambiguous statement of the brutal facts, this undiluted sorrow. Now he would hang up for sure, and no one could blame him.

"Did you *hear* me?" I shrieked.

"Sarah, I'm sorry. I wish . . ."

"What? What do you wish?" Here was hope, hope based on nothing more than an ellipsis, a space for desire to fill.

Just when I had reconciled myself to the silence, he said, very quietly, "I wish I had taken better care of you."

What do you say to that? The very thing you yourself may have been thinking and he says it. How do you hate a man who can come up with something like that? How do you convince yourself that what you called love was not? I felt the hairs rise on my arms, my legs, pulled the T-shirt down over my thighs, bowed my head to my chest. "I know. I know you do."

That night, for the first time in months, I could sleep. I slept through almost until morning, without dreaming. When I woke up I didn't raise the blinds. In that shallow half-light, with my one good eye, I could see his real face. The calm blue eyes so like my sick grandmother's, the heavy nostrils flaring, full lips, those straight white teeth, the ugly mole just beneath his jawline. I don't know why but I decided to let him go. It was at first merely an internal gesture, like intending one person rather than another when you use a common name. But then it gathered momentum. I untied his arms and legs, unlocked the handcuffs with the small key I kept on the chain around my neck, loosened the straitjacket in back, so it no longer looked like he was hugging himself, ripped the masking tape from his mouth-- fast, so it wouldn't hurt. In spite of the ropeburns and the welts, I think he smiled, nodded a thank-you. Is this what love is? Out of gratitude he took a step toward me, looked at me for the first time as if I were human. But before he could open his arms I gave him his heart back. He didn't know how to take what was his. I understand that now. That's why he always laughed so hard at the part in *Midnight Cowboy* where Ratso Rizzo is stuffing the salami into his pockets. That's why he needed me: gifted and greedy. In my imagination I could see him opening outward. I set him free to become whatever he is. Liar, ordinary man, truth-teller I watched him bloom, even in the dark, like a nightflower.

❦

"Sarah?"

"Yes?"

"It's me."

"Where are you?"

"In the slammer, where the fuck do you think?"

I giggled. "Sorry."

"I want you to do something."

"What?"

"I want you to go to my house and get something for me."

"What?"

"Will you do it?"

I knew this trick. "What do you want me to get?" I said again.

"There's a small metal box inside my safe, on the top shelf. No one else has the combination. You're the only one I can trust."

For a moment I was proud of myself. He trusted me. "What's the combination? Did you give it to me? I forget."

"Jesus Christ," he said. "Remember my last divorce? I made you memorize the combination that night we went to Henry K.'s?"

I remembered Henry K.'s. I remembered what I drank that night: Wild Turkey. I remembered the fact of memorizing the combination, but I didn't remember the combination itself. I also didn't want to tell him I didn't remember it.

"Sarah?"

"I'm sorry, Morey, I just don't . . ."

Swearing, snake hissing, ugly sounds coming from the phone for several seconds. Even when he needed me he treated me like this.

I knew he couldn't tell me over the phone. I was that smart, at least. "It'll come to me," I said. In this I had no confidence. "When it does, what do you want me to do? Bring you the metal box?"

"No, stupid. I want you to keep it until I come to get it."

"All right. Can I ask what's in it?"

"You can ask," he said and laughed.

"You're not exactly in a position—" I said and then stopped. It seemed cruel to point out the obvious.

"Not in a position to what?"

"Oh, nothing." I was still afraid of him, even when he was behind bars. I hadn't known that I was so afraid of him and that made me more afraid. What else didn't I know that was crucial to my survival? Maybe I picked men who would hurt me because I missed his man-handling. Maybe I picked men with girlfriends who would put my eye out.

"Morey?" I asked.

"What, honey?"

Do you love me? Is our family going to be all right? "Shall I call you when I've got the box?"

"I can't get incoming calls, dimwit. This isn't a country club." From honey to dimwit in one breath.

"Then I'll write you a letter."

"Are you crazy? What if somebody read it?"

"I got that little thing you wanted. That's what I'll say. All right?"

"You could come to see me."

"Do you want me to?" We had never before had such an intimate conversation. It was mostly good times and torture with nothing in between.

There followed a long silence, as if this would be a great admission of defeat. I heard him take in some breath. Then he said it: "Yes."

"I'll come," I said. "When I've got the box, I'll come."

"Thanks."

"Otherwise how are things going?" Have you got yourself a boyfriend yet? I thought, and smiled a little malicious smile. I knew then that I was not one of the pure in heart.

"I've got to go now," he said. "My time's up."

I said, "I love you," but he had already hung up. Then I wondered if it was true. Did I love him? Or did I only love whoever was my brother and it just happened to be him?

I called Leona Marie the next morning. She picked it up on the first ring.

"Hi, this is Sarah, Morgan's sister." We didn't know each other well. I didn't bother to get to know them since Arlene: they didn't last long, neither the girlfriends nor the wives.

"Yes?" Leona Marie did not believe in smalltalk, for which I admired her, unless I was the one talking to her, and then it made me nervous.

"I talked to Morgan last night," I said, "and he wants me to come over and get something for him out of the safe. Would that be okay?"

"Of course. When would be a good time?"

"How about this afternoon?"

"I'm taking the boys to the doctor for their shots."

"Could you leave the key somewhere I could find it?"

She thought about this for what seemed a long time, as though making a list of what I might want that she had, this being my one opportunity to steal it. "I guess that would be okay. I'll leave the key on the window ledge, in plain sight."

"Thanks." I let there be a silence, but she didn't fill it, and so I felt it my duty to make a fool of myself, to show goodwill. "How are you doing? It must be hard . . ."

"It was hard before this happened. It's easier now with him gone." She said it in a flat reportorial tone.

"Oh." None of the inane things I was prepared to say next were appropriate. Then I couldn't resist. "Do you think he did it?"

"Do I think your brother is capable of killing a woman? Of course. Did he actually do it? I don't know."

"Why did you marry him?"

"Sex, I guess. And all that attention, everybody knowing him wherever we went. Because he was handsome and dazzling. But what was under it was . . . nothing. It took me a long time to believe it, but there's nobody in there."

Was it true? And if it was true, why hadn't I known it? Did I imagine a person in there, with unknown motives and a complicated inner life, as inevitably as you imagined, behind the wheel of a moving car, a driver, behind every natural disaster an angry God?

"Do you know what I found after they arrested him?"

"What?"

"A video camera hidden in the bookcase above the bed. I couldn't sleep one night and I could hear it whirring."

"Why would he—" But I thought I knew. He'd wanted to catch her if she betrayed him. He didn't trust anyone after Arlene.

"I'm sorry," I said. Or maybe he was just carrying on the family tradition. Maybe he wanted his erotic abilities recorded for posterity.

"You didn't do it," she said. "Why should you be sorry?"

She'd cut my sympathy off at the knees and I didn't know what to say. "I'll be over in a couple of hours then. I'll leave the key where I found it. Okay?"

"That'll be fine."

"If you need anything . . ." I felt as if I were speaking to the newly bereaved. I wondered if he had tapes of all the women after Arlene. Or maybe he'd always videotaped himself, even with her, to watch it later, to prove something to himself. What? I once borrowed a book from his room, called *The Magic of Believing*. On the inside cover, in Morgan's curling childish handwriting was the inscription, written over and over, "I who am nothing and should be everything!"

"We don't know each other, Sarah. If I needed anything, I wouldn't ask you for it."

"Of course not," I said. "I was just trying to . . ." Every thought I had after that was more of the same, and finally I just said, "Goodbye," and she hung up without further comment.

Leona Marie was coldly honest. I decided cold honesty was not always a virtue.

I walked out my back door and across the little bridge that stood between Uncle Ad's house and the woods. From there you couldn't even see the other two houses. My grandmother and grandfather had built their house on the other side of the woods, facing away. To give my parents privacy.

It was April and the air was changing. It was warmer, more hopeful. In August the temperature would go above 110 three or four times. But now there were almond blossoms on the trees, and little pockets of light.

When I came out of the woods the sunlight blinded me. The wheat was high and the sky was blue. I thought then that I would never leave this land.

I walked past the place Great Grandmother Blight was buried, near the pond. The grave was marked with a wooden cross whittled by my brother with only her first name on it: Victoria.

There was a wheat field between the woods and my parents' house, with a lone oak tree in the northeast corner. A corn field east of that, all the irrigation pipes coming out of the narrow ditches like animals from the sea, pipes set by Aunt Martha. She was the one who farmed the land now, with the three sons she had by her new husband. My father had another fulltime job: drinking.

The air smelled of freshly cut wheat, though there was no harvester in sight and the wheat was high, so it must have been a memory. I started to cry.

When I walked over the bridge I felt it sway and creak. I jumped up and down on it but this time it didn't give. It seemed dangerous, though we had been driving over it all our lives.

No car in the driveway. No car in the driveway across the creek either. Daddy hadn't come home. I imagined my mother in her chair in front of the TV, smoking her Camels, a small smile of satisfaction on her face. I didn't intend to visit her. I wasn't sure why, but I thought I had to know which side I was on before I saw either Mom or Daddy again. I would have to choose, and I needed more evidence.

I got the key from the ledge in front of the window and opened the door. It was dark in there, all the drapes drawn, in early spring. It made me think of my mother. Maybe they had that in common: the light hurt their eyes.

The safe was on the enclosed porch against the far wall. Eight feet high and six feet wide. I didn't see how anyone could have gotten it into the room. But maybe they built the room around it. It was shiny black, cold and beautiful. My brother sanded it down and painted and repainted it many times as if it were a car.

I spun the dial for practice. Then I tried the combination, my heart beating hard, like a safebreaker come to steal the family treasure.

Sometimes you know things you don't know you know. The heavy black doors swung out into the room. I gasped and fainted backwards, like in the movies. Stacked up on every shelf were bars of gold the size of bricks. Jesus, they must be worth thousands, hundreds of thousands. I wondered if Leona Marie had any idea they were here. But I knew instantly that she didn't. Morgan always had himself set up when he was leaving someone. He never left without coming out better than he'd gone in. That was Morgan's number one rule for living: Do unto others before they do unto you.

I got the small metal box off the top shelf. I sat down on the floor and tried to open it, but it must have been locked. I searched the shelves of the safe for a key but found nothing. On the second shelf was a row of videotapes labeled with women's names. I thought of what Leona Marie had said and knew what they were. On the third shelf were guns, guns of every make and calibre.

I studied the shelves lined with bricks of gold. How much were they worth? I wondered. I considered taking one with me. Probably he wouldn't even miss it, and it would solve every problem I had. Except for the eye. And a man. But with a few hundred thousand I could easily console myself. I thought of Mattie Walker in *Body Heat*. I imagined lying on the beach at Carmel, sipping a Tequila Sunrise, wearing sunglasses, which would not, on a beach, be a sign of cowardice.

I decided to leave the gold for now. I could always come back. And I needed some time to think about whether I could steal from my own brother, and what the chances were of getting caught. If he never got out of jail, for example, the chances would be small or none. I heard my brother's words. "You're the only one I can trust." Poor son of a bitch.

When I got home I put the small metal box on the mantel. I thought of trying to pry open the box with a fork or a knife, but I knew the scratches would be too obvious. I held the box in my lap for a few moments, pressing this way and that, thinking it might spring open at the right touch, but it didn't, so I put it back on the mantel.

I was agitated, restless. I walked all around the living room, touching things—the books on the coffee table, Walker Evans' *Havanna 1933*, Richard Avedon's *In the American West*, a vase my sister had given me with delicate blue flowers on it, a clear glass paperweight shaped like a pyramid—trying to think what to do next.

I picked a spot in front of the TV, clicked it on, and walked back and forth, back and forth. Oprah Winfrey came on. Grief as entertainment. People slobbering all over the microphone. I'll show you my wounds if you show me yours.

"Well, *I* think everyone should be allowed to choose their own lifestyle." Scattered applause. "It's unnatural." A woman with a triple chin and a permanent vertical frown line between her eyes. "If everyone acted that way that would be the end of the human race." Was that a reason for or against? "I didn't choose it, I was born this way," a guest on one of the stage chairs was saying, his hands on his knees, his eyes defiant, impressed with his own boldness. Then a bald guy next to him said, "Nobody forced you. Nobody put a gun to your head. The Bible says it's wrong, pure and simple."

"I'm going to teach you a little game called Russian Roulette. Do you want to play?" Morgan asked.

"Yes."

Right then I was eight years old again and there was a gun to my head.

• •

When I looked down my hands were trembling. Oprah Winfrey was over. A magic act was on, a man dressed in black with a cape like Dracula and a heavily made-up blond in a red-sequinned leotard who was climbing into the box. I looked away as the magician slipped the long knives into the wooden box. I imagined the knives going in, the blond woman bleeding and crying softly, so the audience wouldn't hear, so the magician would not be out of a job on her account. Then I imagined her dead. Afraid of the dark, or of very small spaces, she had died not of knife wounds but of fright, just stopped breathing, like drowning not in water but in your own fear. Who would climb out whole when it was time for the audience to applaud? It was supposed to be magic that she wasn't full of holes, but how amazing is that—avoiding mutilation? And what sane person would put it in a show for kids? What was its meaning?

I turned my mind back toward the gold and felt better almost instantly. My brother owed me that gold, I thought, for all the cruel things he'd done. If I took only one bar of gold for every time he'd humiliated me, beaten me up, scared me to death, made me feel stupid and small, the whole God damn safe would be empty. If someone is evil, were you justified in stealing from him? Mightn't it be a way of restoring order to the universe? Why else was Robin Hood a hero if stealing was wrong?

I turned off the television and got into bed, turned off the light, lay quietly down, arms at my sides, hands open, palms up, trying to relax. I said the combination like a prayer. "Seven, twenty-one, seven, left, right, left," and the movie on my eyelids began, the heavy black doors swung open. I took the bars out of the safe, one by one. They made my elbows ache and my wrists go limp. I worked for half an hour, carefully placing each brick. When I was through I saw the gold laid on every piece of furniture I had—glinting off the dining room table, a short stack on top of the refrigerator, one brick each on the bookshelves in the living room, piled up neatly on the mantel, next to the small metal box, lined up on my chest of drawers, a single bar of gold on my nightstand, a bar of yellow gold on every surface, shining like a thousand eyes in the dark—all the while lamenting my larcenous heart.

THIS IS A PICTURE OF ME, AGE TWO
or three, with wispy red hair, strangling a black cat. I was always hugging a cat, dragging it around by the neck because I was too little to lift it. But Midnight was the one I felt the most affection for. She had shiny black hair and green eyes the size of almonds. She was unusual for a cat in that she would follow me wherever I went. And she could play patty-cake with her paws, just like a real baby.

"He's free?"

"The prosecution's main witness died. The case was dismissed."

"How?" It seemed like cheating. How would we ever know if he'd done it if they didn't have a trial?

"His truck stalled on a railroad track and the train couldn't stop in time."

"Whose truck?"

"The witness."

I thought of Grandfather Blight and wondered whether the engineer had tried to stop, or whether he thought one life was a small price to pay for not having passengers thrown in the aisles, all that Coke spilled over all those green cloth seats.

"He's free?" I said. "You mean he's really free?"

She got a little exasperated. "That's what I just told you, Sarah. They're releasing him tomorrow morning."

"What about Daddy?"

"What do you mean?"

"Is he back home yet?"

"No, he's not. He's probably in a bar somewhere, making friends with a new bottle."

"What are we going to do?" Suddenly I was afraid.

"Do about what? The problem is solved."

No, it's not, I thought. I've got his metal box. I've considered taking his bars of gold.

"Do you think Daddy'll come home now?"

"I don't know, Sarah."

"Is somebody going to pick him up?"

"Your father?"

"No. Morgan."

"Leona Marie is going. She's still his wife."

I nodded. "Well, let me know . . ." Know what? How the movie comes out? Whether the maniac really murdered the beautiful woman? What becomes of the disloyal sister?

"Are you all right?" my mother asked.

"No, I'm not all right," I said. I still had Rich on my mind, and how I should have seen it coming, what I should and should not have said, what I should and should not have done after I said what I should not have said. And my grandmother: the doctor had not called back. I knew I should call Miss Franklin, but there was too much going on in my head, it felt like birdshot in the brain. I kept thinking of Dr. Glass's diagnosis. G-A-D, B-A-D, and a drunk on top of it. And Sunny. I kept seeing Sunny falling.

"Do you want to come over here?" my mother asked.

An invitation to the nuthouse when what you needed was peace. "No, Mama. I'll talk to you later."

When I got off the phone I began a letter to Sunny. *Dear Sunny,* I wrote. *Dear Sunny.* But I didn't know what came next.

Now that Morgan was free he'd be coming soon for the metal box, and I wasn't sure what I wanted my face to look like when he saw it, sympathetic or cold or something in between, inscrutable.

I considered opening the box, which was sure to give me some information. Why else would he have wanted me to get it from his house and let him know when I had? What was in it that he didn't want anyone to see? Then again, who would ever see it when it was locked in his safe and only I had the combination? For and against, for and against.

To see what was inside I would have to pry it open and the results of these efforts would no doubt show on the metal. On the other hand, if he really was a maniac, wouldn't it be better to know it now, before he showed up at my door and began to think of all the little things about me that had irritated him over the years?

I went back and forth like this for a while. It was hard to think of anything as sinister as killing your ex-wife and—. My mind always stopped when it got to that point, what followed the *and,* like someone who stutters, whose mouth stays frozen in the shape of the next word but she can't say it. Arlene in ropes, a human puzzle, her face carefully made up with masking tape and horrified eyes. It began to seem absurd that anyone had even suspected him of such an act. My brother. But they must have had evidence, mustn't they, in order to indict him? Or did they just immediately think of a person's ex-husband as the most likely candidate for a crime of viciousness and malice? Strangers never cared that much, was that the reasoning? For strangers mere swift death was good enough.

I turned off the light and got into bed, tried not to think in the dark. But when I closed my eyes I saw Rich's face in front of me, and I heard him say, "I'll live." I imagined him so vividly that I could smell his aftershave, I could touch his face. And what I prayed for then was to be anything other than the cause of that honorable restraint. I started to scream. I stuffed the corner of the pillow into my mouth and screamed for several minutes, rolled onto my back, cursed the dark and the day I left him.

That's when I decided to take the drugs, in pursuit of unconsciousness, to blot out the night. But I must've gotten up too quickly
because the world went black and I thought I would fall. There I
stood, swooning at the top of the stairs, fumbling for the handrail.
Finally it passed, and on a yellow Post-it pad I made a note to ask Dr.
Glass: Is love too a mere chemical imbalance?

THIS IS ME AGAIN, THE SUMMER I was ten, standing beside the creek with the last gunnysack in my hands, the slight weight of that body. I can see the twenty-five dead cats, one per day, floating stiff-legged on their backs in the bathtub when it was time for my bath. All shot through the head with a .22, a hole the size of a pea. There was surprisingly little blood. I screamed the first time, and the second, and then I didn't scream anymore. But for days after those deaths I found little dark hairs sticking to my skin, like Christmas tree needles you find in the carpet long after the tree has been put out for the garbage men.

THE NEXT MORNING I TOOK THE
metal box and went to stay in my sister's basement. Even her children
didn't know I was there. She came down to visit me that night after
everyone was in bed.

"Do you think he did it?" she whispered. For the last few months
it had been our only topic of conversation. We would try to avoid it
but every time we talked to each other it crept in.

"Do you?"

"I don't know."

I tried to imagine what would constitute proof. A confession. But
that was unlikely. When he was on the police force, he had a reputa-
tion for making prisoners talk, even when they didn't do it. "Send
him to Blight for singing lessons"—that was a saying up at the jail. But
he knew how to keep his own mouth shut. Even when the victim's
skin is under your fingernails, shut the fuck up. I'd heard him say that.

"Suppose he did do it," Angela said. "How would you feel?"

I didn't know. It depended on why he did it, whether it was because she'd betrayed him or because he'd wanted to show her he
could, hurt her because he could, a kind of humiliation, like making
someone say 'Master', like putting a gun to someone's head. It depended on whether he did it on purpose, or whether it was obedience

to something that seemed to come from outside, like grief.

"Would you still love him?" she asked. I thought then that these were the questions she was asking herself. "Would you still think of him as one of us?"

"I never thought of him as one of us. I always thought he was crazy." And then I saw the clear gray eyes of Dr. Glass and remembered the drugs I was taking, and I knew I had no basis on which to make a distinction between my brother and me.

"Remember when he used his magnifying glass to burn up insects on the sidewalk in front of the school?" Angela said. "Remember what a kick he got out of that?"

"I remember." It was a science experiment, to teach the student to focus sunlight on a leaf. As usual Morgan had found another use for it: the torture of small living things.

"I think he did it," Angela said. Then, with more conviction, "He did it, I'm sure of it."

"But you don't have any proof. How do you know?"

"I just know."

"Oh, right. The lightbulb theory of truth. I forgot." Angela believed that whatever you saw clearly and distinctly was true, and that's how we know what we know. No amount of ridicule or reasoning on my part could convince her otherwise.

"Okay," she said, "just say I have *faith* that he did it. How's that?"

"That's progress," I said. "That's probably closer to the truth."

"I'm going to bed. I've got to get up at six in the morning."

I looked at her hard, willing her to stay. In spite of her cracked theories, she had always seemed to me to know something I didn't, to have some equanimity in the face of chaos, the ability to stare past the ruin. I said, "What are we going to do? I still don't know what to do, what to believe."

Angela regarded me with great love and sympathy. She shrugged, shook her head. "Life's a bitch and then you live."

When Angela had gone upstairs I got out a hammer and a screw-driver from the tool chest in her work room and turned the metal box upside down on the coffee table, then wedged the flat-edged tip of the screwdriver between the top and bottom of the box. I aimed at the lock, closed my eyes. But love or terror made me stop.

THAT NIGHT I DREAMED OF UNCLE
Bertie, my mother's brother. We had a coming-out party for Bertie on
the lawn behind the house under the oak trees when he got out of
prison in the summer of 1959. It was August. I was six and I wore my
kelly green dress with the white stretch belt and white sandals. I had
my bathing suit on underneath. I remember the day clearly because it
was the day I ran into the line of barbed wire my father had strung
around the swimming pool to keep the cattle from falling in.

My mother said we should not say words like "jail" or "slammer"
or "murder" or anything else that might remind Uncle Bertie of where
he'd been, what he'd done.

"What did he do?" I asked.

"He killed a man."

"What for?"

"He was in the way. Bertie wanted to leave the bar, and the man
was in the doorway. Bertie asked him to move and the man didn't
move."

"Oh." I thought of Morgan not getting out of my room when I
told him to, even when I screamed, *Get out!* and I understood and
nodded. Kill him.

"What did he kill him with?"

"I don't know," my mother said and frowned as if this were not a question becoming a six-year-old girl.

We spread paper tablecloths on the picnic table and set up the two card tables out on the lawn. My dad brought home a big cable reel from PG&E, and we spread another tablecloth on that. Four tables for all the members of the family. We weighted down each tablecloth with an arrangement of flowers in the middle. Yellow and pink baby roses from my mother's rose garden. We had to borrow three vases from Aunt Martha and I kept pricking my fingers on the thorns. My finger sprung blood and I sucked it until it stopped and I wondered if this was how vampires started out in life.

My mother spent the whole day before the party making potato salad and macaroni salad and fried chicken and home-made banana ice cream in the ice cream maker, just like it was the fourth of July. I liked to run my fingers along the cool shiny iced-up can in which the ice cream was churning, and there was a fluttering in my stomach that I didn't know yet was like being in love. My mother was beautiful that day, with her auburn hair and green eyes. She was wearing a white blouse and white cotton shorts that came up to the tops of her thighs. I asked her if I would look like her when I grew up. She told me again that I was a swan, and one day I would wake up transformed. I waited and waited, peering into the mirror first thing when I got up, asking my mother every morning for several years if it had happened yet. Am I pretty, Mama? But that day I still didn't know that it wasn't going to happen, and it added to the feeling of excitement, the strong sense of possibility, the sense that anything could happen, and that would be the end of the old life, and the new life would have begun.

When I got in bed that night, the movie began on my eyelids: Uncle Bertie in a black leather outfit like I'd seen the Hell's Angels wear when a gang of them roared by on their motorcycles on the highway. Black leather jacket, black leather pants, black boots, silver chains slung here and there like body bracelets. He had black hair and a scar on his face. I fell asleep dreaming that when I turned out to be beautiful Uncle Bertie would take me for a ride on the back of his Harley and we'd drive down the gravel road one evening, just going for a ride, and never come back. I have been haunted all my life— because of Uncle Bertie, perhaps, and my mother's prediction—by dreams of escape and radical change.

Uncle Bertie was a disappointment. Small, puny even. He had the sleeves of his white T-shirt rolled up, a pack of Marlboros tucked into one, and the tops of his arms were no bigger than mine. He had a tattoo of an eagle on his pitiful little bicep. I could have put my hands all the way around it. He walked with a slack butt too, shoulders hunched, as if he'd stood leaning too long against some wall. His face had no scar and no character. Pale blue eyes, flattened nose, no real chin. A plate face. Unforgettably ordinary. And his dirty blond hair was greased back in a ducktail, to show his large flapping ears off to best effect.

He didn't talk much during supper except to say, "This is sure good, we didn't get anything like this in . . ." Then he stopped, looked down, concentrated hard on his plate.

"It's all behind you now," Grandmother Blight said.

I didn't want it to be behind him yet. I wanted to ask him how he'd killed the man. I wanted the details. He didn't look capable of killing anyone. Some people have a lesson to teach you, and I wondered why it was that this was the one thing you were not allowed to ask. My heart started beating hard and I realized I would ask him anyway, in spite of my mother's warning. I could see it beating beneath my green dress and I was afraid someone would see it too and know my plans. I practiced the words under my breath.

"Uncle Bertie?"

He'd say, "What?"

"That man—how did it happen?" To which I hoped he wouldn't say, "What man?" But if he did, I'd say, "The one you . . ." and leave it dangling, maybe slowly drawing my pointer finger across my neck if necessary. Then he'd pantomime the answer for me, so no one would know what question it was the answer to.

After we'd let the ice cream digest for a half hour—house rules—my mother said we could go swimming. I took off my dress right there and ran for the swimming pool at breakneck speed, not paying attention, showing off. It must have looked like something out of a cartoon: I hit the barbed wire right at my neck, sprung backward and smacked the ground with the back of my head. I don't remember crying. They wrapped my neck in a white dishtowel with two thin stripes at one end and took me to the emergency room at the hospital in Manteca. It was nothing serious, the doctor said, though it looked pretty gruesome and I had a big lump on the back of my head where I'd snapped back like the spring on a mouse trap. My biggest regret, though, was that I didn't get to ask my question, and within three weeks Uncle Bertie was back in prison for holding up the liquor store on Wilson Way across from Carter's Auto Supply, and I never got another chance.

In the dream I am trying to speak, to ask my question, but nothing comes out. Uncle Bertie is wearing a kelly green dress with his Marlboros rolled up into one of the sleeves. My mother is in the background, looking at me with disapproval. There is barbed wire around the swimming pool but my neck is still unharmed. This scene is captured in a photograph that is coming to life in the dark room, coming to life in the water beneath my hands. What do I wish to discover? What is it I hope to find? Whether there is something worth killing for, whether he's sorry now, sorry for the life he took or only for the consequences to himself, whether it required great dedication, great courage, or was it an act like being thrown down a well, needing no volition, only the force of a falling object, inevitable once the descent has begun?

WHEN I GOT UP THE NEXT MORNING
I told Angela about the dream. "It was about Uncle Bertie," I said.
"But I think my unconscious was trying to tell me something."

"What?"

"That Morgan did it. That Morgan killed Arlene."

She shook her head. "I just read in the *Atlantic* that Freud got it
wrong. Dreams are electrical impulses the brain shoots off, perfectly
random and arbitrary, the mental garbage of the day. It's like finding an
image in the rain splotches on the ceiling. Even when we're sleeping
we put them together to make the best sense we can. We can't help it."

"What's that? The garbage theory of dreams?"

"You might call it that."

"What about that time Mama dreamed you were sick?" My
mother had woken up one night with the certainty that something
was wrong with Angela because she had dreamed it. Angela was at Cal
at the time, and my mother called her dorm, but no one answered.
When she got hold of her the next morning, Angela had been sick:
her fever had risen above 100 degrees, and she'd been throwing up all
night.

"Coincidence," Angela said with authority.

"And every time a person gets in a car accident their shoes come off." I started to laugh. "And whenever you lose weight, somebody else gains it." I guffawed. "And people always marry someone with a first name of the same number of syllables." I laughed louder. "And you can't die of a disease that hasn't been discovered yet." I fell on the floor laughing. "And when you get through praying tonight, your husband will be a lot nicer, he'll probably start doing the God damn dishes and kissing your long skinny toes." I laughed so hard I couldn't breathe.

Angela looked hurt. "Go ahead, make fun," she said. "I know what I know."

"Oh, that's right. We wouldn't want to forget your finest achievement. The lightbulb theory of truth."

"Maybe the mistake is to expect proof," Angela said. "Maybe doubt is always reasonable."

I thought of the woman I had seen on Oprah Winfrey last week, whose husband had blindfolded and gagged her, tied her up to the four-poster bed, played a knife over her breasts, then "made love" to her, all captured on video, the woman pleading and crying, the woman screaming in terror. The jury said the husband was not guilty, eight women and four men. How could you rape your own wife? How could you steal your own dog? That's the day I gave up trash TV.

I didn't tell Angela what I was thinking. I knew it was an image she wouldn't want in her head. Neither did I. But what are we to do, who hope to face the truth?

After breakfast, I went back downstairs and studied the box, holding it in my lap like a child, rocking. Why didn't I open it? What prevented me? Was I afraid of what my brother would do when he found out? Or was I afraid of what he had already done? Either way there was something to be afraid of. But what good would it do to know if he'd killed Arlene? If I didn't believe in his innocence enough not to open the box, then finding evidence he didn't do it wouldn't be loyalty at all but something else, like loving somebody because he bought you presents. Every move I could make seemed to mean something I didn't want to believe about myself, but something I might need to know if I wanted to live.

THIS IS A SNAPSHOT OF THE LAST
survivor.

On the twenty-fifth day, I hid Midnight in the outhouse that
stood at the edge of the woods. I made the cat a bed of rags in a white
porcelain pan that I set in the hole that was used for a toilet long ago.
I set a dish of milk on the outhouse floor, along with a bowl of
Friskies. I left my jacks and a small red rubber ball so she would have
something to amuse her. I locked the door of the outhouse with the
combination lock from my fourth-grade school locker. Every day
after school, all that week, I would lag behind my eighth-grade
brother and fifth-grade sister, kicking gravel, skipping rocks in the
creek, so they would get impatient and go ahead, and I could make
sure Midnight was safe before going home.

WHEN I WENT BACK TO THE RANCH the next day to get some clean clothes there was a blinking red light on my answering machine. I expected a message from Morgan. I knew what it would say. "If I don't have that metal box by nightfall, bitch, you're dead meat." I punched the button and felt my heart beating hard.

"I forgive you." My ex-husband's voice. Forgiveness in the midst of chaos and betrayal and the threat of death.

I called Rich at work and they said they'd page him. I sat down by the telephone to wait.

I don't know why this particular memory should come back, why sex and forgiveness were somehow connected in my mind, but I thought of the year we lived in Portland, the day we knocked down the shower walls making love.

When Rich came on the line his voice sounded hoarse as if he'd been remembering the same thing.

I said, "What's wrong?"

"Nothing, sweetie. How're you doing?" I heard what sounded like a saw screaming in the background.

"Okay. I'm okay."

There was a moment of silence because I wanted to say something about his message but I didn't know what to say, everything I could think of seemed unworthy.

"Is anybody there?" I asked. I knew it didn't make any sense, but I didn't want anyone to hear.

"A couple of guys, but they're not paying any attention," he said. "Besides, you can't hear the other end of the conversation except in movies."

I laughed.

"So what's up?"

I started to tell him some inconsequential things, like getting my finger stuck in the coffee grinder. The lid was cracked and when I put it back on I caught my little finger in it. While the small grinder whirred, slicing into my finger, and I yanked to get my finger out, yelling and cursing, I thought of Morgan pulling my hair, how if I tried to pull away it hurt more, but if I leaned toward the pain it hurt less, and as soon as I quit yanking to get it out, the cracked plastic let go of my finger.

"You always were accident prone. Remember that time you totaled your mother's car?"

"Which one?" I had an image of all the cars I'd totaled lined up in a row. A black Studebaker, a red Bonneville, a gold GTO, a borrowed Thunderbird, and a beat-up Eldorado, which is all they'd let me drive my last year of high school. Enough to start my own junk yard.

"You were hell on cars." He laughed. "And men."

"How's Sunny?" I asked to change the subject. "I mean, Michael. How's Michael?"

"I love that kid," he said. "We're buddies. I feel like, with him, I can make up . . . for some of the mistakes I made with Sunny."

I said, "Maybe you can."

I told him I was considering getting a black patch and wanted his opinion. "Everyone needs an advisor," I said. "What do you think? Would it be selling out? Or just common sense?"

"I can't imagine you with a black patch. I've never made love to a woman with a black patch." He laughed. "I bet that would be a new experience. Maybe it would make me feel like a Viking."

I laughed. "It'd still be me," I said. "Me in a black patch."

"That's more than enough for me."

When I'd run out of smalltalk I couldn't put it off anymore. I said, "I got your message," but my voice came out small, and I wasn't sure if he'd heard me so I said it again, and this time I said it too loudly. *"I got your message."*

For a long time there was silence. Then he said, "I know."

THIS IS A PICTURE OF THE BLACK-
berry bush that grew by the well, three tangled branches rising from a
stump.

When I got home from school that day the lock on the outhouse
was off, the door was open, and my cat was gone. On the floor he'd
made an *M* with the jacks, to let me know it hadn't happened by
chance. I ran all the way home, in through the front door of the house
and out the back, yelling his name. I found him by the well, near the
blackberry bush that had been chopped down by my father five or six
times but always grew back. Every summer my mother made blackberry pies, sheet pies that covered two large cookie pans, and said,
"That blackberry bush may be our only imitation of immortality."

Morgan was standing by the well, looking down, his arms crossed
over his chest with satisfaction. "Would you like to make a wish?"

"What did you do with Midnight?"

He gestured with his head toward the well. "She seems to have
had a little accident." He sounded genuinely concerned.

I looked down into the well, which was dry at that time of the
year, and there was Midnight peering up, mewling pathetically.

I jumped up and down, yelling and flinging my hands in the direction of the well, "Get her out! Get her out! GET. HER. OUT!"

"Don't get hysterical," he said calmly. "I have a little proposal for you. A little proposition I think might interest you."

I waited.

"You know how you're always saying, 'Let me do it'? Well, this time I'm going to let you."

I waited, still not understanding.

"Just to show how much I like you, I'm going to let you kill your own cat."

"I won't. You can't make me."

"I've got a little Colt .22 right here that should do the job nicely. It only holds one bullet. One little bullet for one little black cat. So you better not miss."

He handed me the gun, and I dropped it very close to the edge of the well as if it were hot.

"Pick it up," he said, grabbing my hair in a fist at the back of my head, forcing me to my knees. "That's it. That's much better. Now stand up."

I stood at the edge of the well, looking down, his hand still twisted in my hair. "Now pull the hammer back."

The gun was very small—less than four inches long—and it fit easily in my small hand, like I was made for it. I felt a little chill that raised the hair on the back of my neck as I pulled back the hammer—first one click, then another.

"Good. For a girl, you catch on very quickly." He smiled. "Now all you have to do is pull the trigger. When you're ready."

I squinted my left eye, and got the cat in the sight of the gun with my right.

"Hurry up. I haven't got all day. I'm an important guy, you know. I've got places to go, people to do." He laughed his ugly laugh, pleased with the appropriateness of the phrase he'd been repeating for weeks.

I moved the barrel of the gun slightly to the left and fired. The cat screamed, jumped straight up in the air, and came down on four feet, unharmed.

"I *told* you we only had one bullet. I told you not to miss. Look what a mess you've gotten us into *now*, Ollie." He fluttered the imaginary tie at his neck and then cracked up at his own impression. "Laugh," he said sternly. "You're too serious. I've been meaning to talk to you about that. You've got to learn to see the humor in the situation."

He still had hold of my hair. I laughed half-heartedly.

"That's better," he said cheerfully. "Now what?" He seemed to be thinking. He seemed genuinely not to know what came next.

That's when I stomped on his instep and jammed my elbow into his ribs, saying, "No, no, no, no." In the brief altercation that followed, he threw me down the well and as I hit bottom I broke the neck of Midnight.

THE NEXT TIME I SAW MY GRAND-
mother was at her funeral. The whole family came.

I sat between Angela and my mother in the frontmost pew on the
left. My brother sat behind us, with a woman I didn't know: bleached
blond, stacked, long legs, money. My father sat in the frontmost pew
on the other side, with Aunt Martha.

The church was less than half full. Most of the people who'd loved
my grandmother had already died. In two ways she'd died too late.
But then because of the first way—her mind going—I guess it didn't
matter that her friends weren't there. It was all family, except for the
old man in the wheelchair, parked at the end of the third row. Harold,
I think his name was. His head bobbed back and forth like it was sitting on top of something unstable, like a plate on a stick.

The organ music played softly as people straggled in. "Shepherd
Show Me How to Go." I hummed a little to myself, thinking how little I'd learned in this year of my undoing.

My brother said, apparently having meditated on this before
speaking, "You treat her better now that she's dead than when she was
alive." Referring to the expensive casket, I suppose, silk and gold, all
those flowers. "When she was alive you didn't even deign to visit her."
Deign was said with great contempt. It sounded odd, like a little kid

trying out a new word to impress somebody.

My mother answered him back although he was speaking directly to our father, across the aisle and one row up from Morgan, speaking to the back of his head. "And I suppose you did visit?" she shrilled at him. "I suppose you are just oh so morally superior to the rest of us?" She seemed to be angry at the price she'd paid for standing up for him—Daddy on the other side of the aisle, her life in ruins.

And without the slightest hesitation he said, "I didn't betray her at least. I didn't sell her down the river. And yes, I did go to see her. I went every Sunday," he said, "except when I was . . . in prison. I never saw any of you there." His chin jutted out on *you*.

I said, in my defense, "I went at night," though it was true I had not gone in many nights. And I hadn't called Miss Franklin back, or the doctor who had put her in the hospital.

He put his hand on my shoulder, to let me know he'd heard. Then he glared across the aisle at my father. "Was drinking so important?" he asked. "She was your *mother*, for Christ sake!" Then he glared at his own mother. "Was your big-screen TV so important? That *crap* you read?"

My mother started to cry. "You know I can't —" she said and then stopped. Because here she was, proof that she could, if it meant enough.

It was his self-righteousness, more than anything, that made me think he didn't kill Arlene. You couldn't be self-righteous about visiting your grandmother, could you, if you'd killed and trashed your third ex-wife? Then again, Arlene had betrayed him, and maybe he thought that made it okay. My brother had never learned the art of self-doubt. He'd never questioned his nature, merely expressed it. Then maybe his self-righteousness was proof not of his innocence but of his guilt. Perhaps in his book some things did not merit forgiveness but rather death. What Arlene had done to Morgan? What Morgan had done to Arlene? What I had done to my ex-husband? What Jake had done to me? What we had done to Morey, suspecting him, shutting him out?

How much sense does it make anyway? Proof. You can't prove most of the important things in life—whether, for instance, there is even a point to living. Maybe you were doing someone a favor by killing her. Had anyone investigated that? Why is killing so bad anyway, if someone is evil, and you know it? Because we're not sure they're evil, and somebody might decide we're evil and try to kill us, and that's what we want protection against, so we agree not to kill anyone else, so no one will kill us. Self-interest after all, nothing more?

I didn't know the truth, and in the meantime I had to live.

"I loved her," I said too loudly for a church, and my mother turned and looked directly into my face, startled at first, then nodding in agreement.

"I loved her too," she said, her voice strong.

And then Angela said it, "I loved her," and there followed a chorus, like those Christmas hymns in which the soprano answers the bass, and the alto answers the soprano. "I loved her." Then another voice, "I loved her," and another, "I loved her." And the old man said it too. The organ player pressed down on his pedal and raised his hands higher and came down harder so as to rise above the voices, but the chorus grew louder, and I thought that even though our grandmother had died too late she had died at the right time.

On the way to the cemetery Morgan sat beside me in the car following the hearse and whispered, "Did you get it?"

"What?" I said and began to hum an old hymn from childhood.

"The box."

I looked out the window at the winter-dry fields of wheat stubble, down the rutted road that led to the cemetery.

"I got it," I said, and continued to hum.

When I got home from the cemetery Rich was there. Morgan drove up behind me in his red Maserati and got out of the car. He touched my shoulder and shook his head, so I guessed he didn't want me to give him the metal box in front of Rich.

"Angela called me," Rich said in explanation.

Morgan and Rich shook hands.

"How're you doing?" Rich asked.

"As many as I can," Morgan said. "The easy ones twice."

"That's Grandma's saying, not yours," I said to him with great contempt. "Don't use it again."

"Fuck you, sweetie," he said and smiled. "Catch you later." He slapped my face twice, just lightly.

He left a cloud of dust behind him as he drove off down the gravel road, and I wished this was the end of the movie.

"How did you get away?" I asked Rich.

"I said I was going to Great Falls."

"I'm glad you came." I took his hand and led him into the house. We sat on the couch, holding hands, and told stories about my grandmother.

Rich had loved my grandmother too. When she was seventy years old, she came to visit us in Alaska, and he'd bought her an acre of Alaskan wilderness, the deed printed on a certificate with her name on it. When he handed it to her I thought the smile would split her face. He bought her a gold pan and took her to the Salmon River to pan for gold and even managed to slip some gold nuggets into the wash for her to find.

"I always liked Rich," she said to me whenever we got on the subject of my past. "I could never understand why you left him. Of all the men in our family, I always thought he was the best built." As if there were only one reason to leave a man.

Even in the last year of her life, my grandmother was the object of male desire. About a year ago when I went to visit her she said in a whisper, "Harold, the man in the wheelchair, tried to kiss me." Then she laughed and shrugged her shoulders in girlish embarrassment as if to say, What can you do? It's not my fault if they want me. From then on I'd tease her. "Has Harold been in today?" I'd ask and she'd giggle. Eighty-seven years old and still getting propositions.

I told Rich this story, and the story of Uncle Ad and the World's Fair, and all the other stories I could remember, and he listened like he'd never heard any of them before.

I didn't tell him about Morgan, or about Mom and Daddy splitting up. We didn't talk about Sunny. It was as if we had just met but had known each other forever. I had a vivid sense that our life was beginning again.

"Remember that time in Portland?" he said as if he were thinking the same thing. "Remember how we knocked down the shower walls?"

"I remember. I had just stepped into the shower when you walked in. You said, Sarah? Can I come in? I'm really dirty. I don't think I can wait." I laughed and kissed him. "I said, Okay."

"I opened the glass door, and you watched me take off my Levis and unbutton my shirt. I remember your wet hair clear down your back." He unzipped my dress while he talked. "I stepped in. I said, Do you need a little help with that soap? The places you can't reach? And you handed me the soap." He helped me take off my black dress, and then I undressed him, first the shirt unbuttoned slowly from the bottom.

"First you moved it over my breasts, in a circular motion, like this, then around to my back, starting at my shoulders and moving down. Then you kneeled and soaped my legs, beginning at my feet, picking up one foot, then the other, taking your time, and when you did the bottoms of my feet I remember it tickled, and then you moved on to my calfs, coming up slowly, inch by inch."

"Like this?" he said.

"Yes. Like that." He kneeled at my feet. "By the time you got to the tops of my thighs I couldn't wait."

He pulled me up from the couch and lifted me, remembering what came next.

"You picked me up and I wrapped my legs around your waist, but the soap made me slippery and just when the rhythm was good, when everything was right, I'd slip from your hands."

He laughed. "I remember."

"You picked me up again, and again I slipped, down to the bottom of the shower, the water running in my face."

"This time I've got you," he said, backing me up against the wall.

"The next time you picked me up, you backed me into a corner of the shower, and began again, taking it slow, and with you inside me and the warm water running in my mouth, it felt like the first time we made love, remember, how my heart was beating so hard you could hear it, and I couldn't breathe?"

"I remember." He was kissing me and trying to talk at the same time. "When I heard the first tile give I didn't know what it was," he said, moving against me. "Then the second one fell, and then a whole row dropped onto the floor of the shower, just missing my feet."

"I remember we both laughed, but we didn't stop making love, and by the time we were through, the water was cold and the shower was destroyed, two whole walls caved in, the wallboard wet, in pieces, tile all over the shower floor."

"Here," he said. "That's it."

"The best part is what you said when we got the bill for over four hundred dollars."

"What? I don't—"

"We were sitting at the kitchen table, remember? You opened the envelope and flinched. I said, What's the damage? And you ripped it in half and said, 'It was worth it.'"

He said, "It is."

The sun cut through the curtains and laid a strip of light across the bed.

"When I saw you standing there in front of the mirror last night, combing your hair before you came over here to lay down beside me . . . I fell in love with you again."

"I feel the same way," I said. "Like everything is new."

He laid his hand on my bare stomach. "Why did you leave me? I always wanted to know but I didn't think I had the right to ask."

It was something I had never been able to face. Walking out like that. No warning, no explanation. It was right after The Summer of Men. Even then I knew it didn't make any sense, it wasn't fair, but I thought, What kind of man would have a wife like that, a wife who could go through thirty men in one summer without batting an eye?

Not a man you could respect. Not a man you would want to be married to.

"You wouldn't dance," I said.

He laughed, but then looked at me confused, right at the edge of angry.

"Remember that time at Gilley's and you kept saying, 'In a minute,' and we sat there for three hours and you still wouldn't dance, and you wouldn't let me dance with anyone else who asked me, and I started crying into my Tequila Sunrise?"

"I don't remember."

"I wasn't crying because you wouldn't dance. I remember thinking that I was no longer that person, the kind of person who *would* cry because her husband wouldn't dance with her. And *that's* what made me cry."

"Nobody leaves somebody because they won't dance, for Christ sake."

"Maybe you're right," I said. I tried to think of a better reason for leaving. "Anything I said would just be . . . made up. After the fact. Like finding an image in the rain splotches on the ceiling."

"It would help me to know." He didn't say it in a tone of self-pity but with dignity. "Maybe then I could let go."

"I don't want you to let go."

He nodded and pulled me close to him, like it was all settled, with just those words.

"For years I thought about you every night," he said. "It was like having the same dream over and over. I kept seeing your hair in the sunlight. Isn't that the damnedest thing? Your hair."

I held his hand.

Then I guessed he remembered something about her, because he said, "Let's think it over. The world is full of people doing what they want, and look at the shape it's in. I made a promise. I don't know if I can go back on it, even for this. I don't know if I can do that to them." He studied my face for a moment and I hoped he wasn't seeing my eye.

"The world is full of people doing what they're sup*posed* to do," I said, "when their heart's not in it. It takes guts to do what you want." I thought about this and wondered whether I believed it. "You wouldn't even have that kid if I hadn't left you. Think about that."

He smiled. "I always did want him to know you, to know what you're like."

"This way he would," I said. "I'd get to have . . . an influence on him." I'm not like her, I thought. It would be good for his son to know a woman who was not a doormat.

He nodded.

"I wouldn't wait on you like she does," I said. "You better think about that. I don't cook. I don't wash anybody's clothes except my own. In case you've forgotten."

He laughed. "I haven't," he said. "You were shit for a wife."

Suddenly he seemed alien, somebody I didn't know. Shit for a wife. I was. And I'd be shit for a second wife too.

"Well, maybe we better not rush into anything," I said. "It's a big step. You have your son to think of. And your *wife*." The word came out as a sneer.

"Let's sleep on it," he said, putting his arm around me, pulling me to him. But I felt far away from him right then, and I didn't want to sleep on it.

"I've got to get back," I said. "I've been staying at Angela's."

He didn't ask why and I didn't offer an explanation.

"Let's do it this way," he said. "If we really want to be together again, we'll send each other a Christmas present. As a message."

"Like what?"

"I don't know." He thought a moment. "Something from the past?"

"Okay," I said. "That's a good idea."

I got up from the bed and started to dress.

"I always loved watching you," he said. "Every move you make."

There would be problems, of course, but we'd work them out. We had a whole history together. Where could you find another man who had loved you since you were seventeen?

By the time I was in the car we were together again in my imagination. He leaned in the window and kissed me.

"Nothing in the world would make me happier," he said, putting his hand through the open window.

I touched his forearm and it seemed precious, just the direction of the hairs, his familiarity, his unquestioned love of me. It made perfect sense, didn't it, my life coming in a circle, getting my family back, what was lost not mattering?

"Nothing."

"Mama just called. She wanted
to know if I'd seen you. She said she'd been calling you all morning."

"What did she want?"

"The land has been put up for sale," Angela said. "A real estate
agent came this morning and Mama signed the papers."

"Why?"

"She said it was because she didn't want to stay out there all alone,
with Daddy gone, but I don't think that was it."

"What then?"

"I think she wanted to punish Daddy for not believing in Morgan, for not believing what she believed. And I think she wanted to
punish Morgan, for what he said at the funeral, for blaming her for
not going to visit Grandmother Blight."

I nodded. It made sense. The big house was supposed to have
been Morgan's when Mom and Daddy died. Over the years he'd done
a lot of work on it—putting on a new roof, building a sun porch, a
new and larger picture window in the front, digging the pond, plant-
ing the weeping willows along the creek. This would be a good way
of expressing her disapproval, of showing him she was not an old
woman who couldn't leave her house, but someone to be reckoned
with.

"But Daddy has to sign too, doesn't he? She can't just sell it out from under him."

"No, but she can get him to sign, you know that won't be hard. She's gotten him to do whatever she wants all her life."

"What about me? Where will I go?" The land up for sale. The land that had been ours for six generations, seven counting Sunny. It was something I thought I could count on, that would always be mine, a place for me to be.

"You can always live here," Angela said, putting her arm around me.

"In the basement?"

I banged the handle of the screwdriver with the hammer and the box flew across the room. I retrieved it and tried again. This time I sat on the coffee table with my thighs around the box so it wouldn't go anywhere. When I pounded this time on the handle end of the screwdriver the box pinched the skin of my thighs and I yelled out, "God damn *son* of a bitch!" and immediately thought of my father, and wondered where he was, how he could believe this of his son.

I pounded again and this time the point of the screwdriver went through the coffee table, leaving splinters of oak veneer stuck in my thighs. Instead of crying, wailing out my rage at the injustice of the world that would let such things happen to me, I picked the splinters out carefully and returned to my task, intent on knowing, willing to pay the price. At the next assault the box was lying on the rug, its contents spilled out and although my success had admittedly not been elegant, it was nonetheless success.

There were three snapshots and a two-carat diamond ring. One picture was of Arlene in all her glory lying on what looked like a black silk bedspread, her left hand on her thigh, her shoulder bent toward her chin, the ring on her hand. *Morticia in Love.* One was of Arlene when she was nine or ten and not the age she was when she died, thirty-five. In the picture her teeth are in braces, her arms and legs too long and skinny, and the look on her face is of a child who needs my help, though she is now beyond it. The third picture was of our family, one I'd seen many times, a standing portrait with my mother and father in back, Morgan and Angela in front of them, and me in front of Morgan and Angela. Angela's hair is in pipe curls and she is smiling, beautiful beloved child. Morgan and I are either skeptical of this happy family portrait or squinting into the sun. My mother's face is serious, perhaps she's considering a divorce. My father is staring off to the right, apparently distracted by something beyond the edge of the picture, in love with the photographer's assistant or a bottle of Chivas waiting in the wings.

My sister came down the stairs. "What's going on?" she said. "It sounds like you're dismantling the house." She looked at the splintered coffee table and her face fell.

I said, "I'm sorry. I was trying to open something, and it wouldn't come." I was sitting on the box.

"It's three in the morning," Angela said. "Maybe you'd better give it up for the night. If you don't want the whole family down here."

I said all right. I said I'd go to sleep.

She came over and kissed me good night, to show she didn't care about the coffee table, to show people were more important than splintered oak. I thought then that if it had been my coffee table, I'd have been screaming my head off, talking about respect for other people's property, eliciting promises of replacement or compensation, figuring the tax. The differences between Angela and me were great, and it made me ashamed.

After Angela had gone back upstairs, I studied the contents of the box, all laid out on the dark gray carpet. Nothing that seemed to mean anything. I speculated briefly on how much you could get for a slightly used two-carat diamond ring.

I put the pictures and the ring back into the box and tried to re-lock it, but the lock had been broken by the hammer-and-screwdriver stunt. My heart was beating in my face. What would I say when he found out where I was staying and demanded the metal box? I would lie and say I'd never gotten it out of the safe; I lied and told him I had because I was afraid he'd be mad at me. I tried, of course I tried, knowing how important it was to him but could not remember the combination. Stupid me. That was more plausible really than what had happened, the black doors swinging open at the combination I'd guessed. But would he believe me, when I'd told him after the funeral that I had it? Of course he could look in the safe himself and then he wouldn't believe me because the box would be gone. I could say Leona Marie had taken it. Boy, were you right, I'd say, the bitch, she just knocked me over, took the God damn box and ran. And then what would he do? Or I? That's when I saw it—the little frayed cor-ner of the red velvet—and I pulled on it, but it wouldn't come up. I used the tip of the screwdriver to pry it loose. Under the red velvet there was a false bottom to the box. I worked on it for several minutes without success, turning it this way and that, shaking it, peering in-side, looking for the trick, the heat rising in my face. Finally, I saw a small metal catch, no larger than the button you use to set the clock on the car radio. I pressed it and nothing happened. Then I used the tip of my fingernail and it sprang up, like a Jack-in-the-Box when the song is done. Under the false bottom was a video tape titled *Arlene*.

Angela didn't have a VCR so I would have to go home if I wanted to see it. But then he might be there, and I was pretty sure he wouldn't want to make popcorn and sit down with me to watch.

I felt a screaming in my brain but I couldn't tell anyone what I'd found, without the choice I would make thereby being decided, and I wanted to make this choice alone, with great deliberation, because I thought even then that it was a choice of the greatest importance, deciding as it did the priority of two considerable things, and the consequences, though unimaginable, would continue to the end of the part of the world we called our lives, maybe further, if the as-yet-undreamed grandchildren should hear the story and, hearing it, labor to understand how it altered both the future and the past, their very conception of themselves.

THIS IS A PORTRAIT OF A GRAVE, with the name of the beloved carved with an ice pick on the back of a broken yardstick. *Midnight.* My mother helped me to dig it with the same shovel we used to plant the flowers that grew in a circle around the tall oak tree, the one with the ledge for sitting in the sun. We laid a hundred of my mother's yellow roses on top of the grave—it was important to me that there be exactly one hundred—and Angela stood there weeping, all dressed in white, her lips moving in prayer. "The Lord Thy God my Master is, His goodness faileth never. I nothing lack for I am His, and He is mine forever." My mother read one of her favorite poems, "The Second Coming."

> Turning and turning in the widening gyre
> The falcon cannot hear the falconer;
> Things fall apart; the centre cannot hold;
> Mere anarchy is loosed upon the world,
> The blood-dimmed tide is loosed, and everywhere
> The ceremony of innocence is drowned;
> The best lack all conviction, while the worst
> Are full of passionate intensity.
> Surely some revelation is at hand;

Surely the Second Coming is at hand.
The Second Coming! Hardly are those words out
When a vast image out of *Spiritus Mundi*
Troubles my sight: somewhere in the sands of the desert
A shape with lion body and the head of a man,
A gaze blank and pitiless as the sun,
Is moving its slow thighs, while all about it
Reel shadows of the indignant desert birds.
The darkness drops again; but now I know
That twenty centuries of stony sleep
Were vexed to nightmare by a rocking cradle,
And what rough beast, its hour come round at last,
Slouches towards Bethlehem to be born?

We held hands in a circle around the grave, and then I took this picture, *Elegy for Midnight*. So I would never forget. Looking back, that was the real beginning of my career.

When the service was over I asked, "Where is she now? Did she go to heaven?" My mother took me in her arms and rocked me. She smoothed my hair. She whispered, "I'm sorry, Sarah, I'm sorry, Sarah, I'm so sorry, Sarah." By which I took her to mean *No*.

"IT WAS LIKE SOMEONE VERY heavy had been standing on my neck," I said, bowing my head, indicating where he might have been standing, "and this morning he got off."

Dr. Glass nodded.

"No. That's not quite right. I felt the way you do when you first fall in love, like anything's possible, now my real life would begin."

"Mm-hmm."

I cleared my throat, tried again. "It was like Christmas had come in the middle of the night. The air around my bed felt colder, less stifling." The angle of the blinds made a pattern of light on the dark blue comforter, and it seemed like a revelation, a truth that went right through you. I tried to explain it.

"I put my bare feet on the floor, one at a time, and I was aware of the texture of the wood beneath my feet, my hands were alien objects, strange and handsome." I held them up for her inspection, waving the fingers like little ghosts.

Dr. Glass nodded.

"I went downstairs, and the yellow porcelain teapot I used to boil water in seemed strikingly beautiful. I went to look in the mirror to see if my face had been magically transformed. My eye was still gone but it wasn't a tragedy. A disfigurement, that's all. Something people might not notice on the street unless they were rudely staring into other people's faces. It looked like I was winking, like I had a great secret."

She nodded. "What then?"

"I turned on some music. Aretha Franklin. I was wearing Jake's T-shirt that came down to the middle of my thighs. I danced around on the wooden floor in my bare feet. Aretha was singing 'A Change Is Gonna Come' and she was singing it for me."

Dr. Glass looked up, the tactful equivalent of rolling her eyes; she put her lips together like she was blotting lipstick. A look titled How to Handle a Lunatic.

"I took off the T-shirt and threw it in the corner, and I could not stop dancing. The blood sang in my veins and without the need of prayer or renunciation of the flesh," I said, my voice rising higher and higher, "I felt I had been saved."

More polite eyerolling. But the color was rising in her cheeks, her gray eyes were feverish, bright.

"I took my Leica out of its case. I wanted to be able to recall this feeling at will, and pictures had always helped me to bring back the past. I put the camera on its tripod, set the self-timer, and took a picture of me rising from my bed, throwing back the covers, stretching. *Coming to Life.* I took a picture of my bare feet against the oak slats of the floor. The white white skin, the hideous long toes, the red bumps on each side and at the heel seemed touching, worthy of contemplation. *The Healing of Feet.* I took a picture of the light through the blinds, the pattern it made on the dark blue comforter, the shadow of a human body on the sheets, the shape it left. *After.* I stood with my back to the camera, held the picture of the dancer on the rock in front of my face, looked into it, and the darkness of the rock blotted out the loss of my eye, and reflected back my real face. *Dancer with Bruised Knees.* I wanted to develop the film right then, to give the prints away, to show someone the way the world looked the morning my life changed. But I couldn't concentrate. My hands shook, I was so happy."

"The medication," Dr. Glass said. "It happens this way for some of my clients. The depression lifts abruptly." She smiled, a smile that took all the credit, a smile that held the patent.

"The drugs?" I said. The drugs had kicked in. "Is this life as the normal live it?"

"Well, not being able to step inside your skin . . ."

I felt stopped by happiness, unable to proceed. "You mean this is how I'm going to feel, from now on?"

"Maybe on Christmas and New Year's Eve," she said. "I wouldn't count on it."

I couldn't sit still. I said, "I have to go. Goodbye. Thank you!" I gave her a hug—a hug! this rigid woman I had never touched—and walked out the door.

I punched the DOWN arrow at the elevator, smiling to myself in the double mirrors. Not bad, I thought. Not bad for a one-eyed woman who's almost 40.

On the ride down to the first floor I snapped my fingers and tapped my toes. I sang, "Come on, Baby, let the good times roll."

Then I felt someone staring at me. Who should it be? My old friend from the Wayside Nursing Home, Mr. Meese.

I nodded in greeting as if he were possibly human and to my surprise he nodded back.

On the ride down, he stood well away from me and I saw the muscle in his jaw clenched and the skin inside his chin dimple was white but he didn't scream or bolt when the doors opened.

"Goodbye," I said with a certain dignity, as if whether he

responded or not were a matter of complete indifference.

He looked back at me with a look halfway between fear and goodwill (scared eyes and a slight smile) but said nothing. I watched him go, one pantleg hitched up at the top of his black hightop tennis shoes, giving him a lopsided jaunty look, and although the year had been dismal I felt hopeful, felt that here in the person of this pale ordinary man was moral progress.

I stood outside the elevator watching it make its slow ascent to the top of the building. 5. 6. 7. I looked around but no one was coming. Watching myself in the mirror, I kicked my right leg up as close as I could to my ear while flinging my arms into the air. I heard something rip. So I bunched up my pants at the tops of my thighs to get a little more kicking room and tried the maneuver again. This time I fell flat on my ass due to the slickly waxed floors. I got up and tried it again. The arms were all right—quite elegant, in fact—but the leg was the wrong angle, not high enough. I practiced the kick over and over until I had come as close as possible to the woman in the picture.

I saw him coming.

I was walking over to the big house to try to talk Mama out of selling the land, snapping pictures all the way, in rapid succession, in case I failed: with a portfolio of the past I would be ready for grief. I moved up the creek, across the lawn, and dwelled on the rose garden. It stood where the old swimming pool had been filled in, a long bench of seating all around the edge, as if watching rosebushes were a popular sport or rite in a new religion. I took three shots of the life-guard station made of railroad ties, its legs dug deep in mud. It looked like a medieval throne, just after the abdication. Then one of the house, from a distance, going away. Shades of green—tree, grass, weed—more stubbled field where my father farmed when we were children, all against a flat blue sky. A shot of the fig tree, bare in winter, its grasping branches. One of the leaning outhouse, its warped boards gray and rotting. One of the blackberry bush that grew from the stump by the wishing well. Then, hanging as far as I could over the brick-laid edge, I took one dark shot of the bottom. I set the camera down, right there beside the well.

It began as a billow of dust at the end of the gravel road. I don't know how I knew but I started running. By the time I got to my mother's back yard he had knocked down the tall oak tree near the swimming pool, which must have been rotten inside, it fell so easily.

He ran the bulldozer into the grape arbor, again and again. The grinding of the gears of the machine was deafening. He lifted out whole rose bushes from the filled-in swimming pool. Three of the bushes that had been ripped out lay on the ground. They looked like slaughtered aliens.

My mother came running out of the house and tried to reason with him. "What are you doing?" she screamed.

"I'm taking what's mine." He raised the bucket on the bulldozer and ran it into the roof over the patio, then knocked down the glass patio doors. The glass fell in great slabs, unsplintered.

My mother was shaking so badly I thought she was going to collapse. "Morey!" she screamed. "Morey. It's *us!*" As if he couldn't see.

He backed the bulldozer up and headed away from the house, toward the pond.

"Let's get out of here," I said. "Let's leave." I took her by the elbow but she didn't budge. "We can't do anything to stop him," I said. "Let's go! Mama! *Please!*"

She said, "I can't." She ran back into the house, and I followed her.

She went to the wall telephone by the built-in desk between the living room and kitchen. "I'm going to call your father, he'll know what to do," she said, a thought she had never expressed in the nearly forty years I had known her.

I looked up the number for her, flipping the pages too quickly, ripping them, my hands slick with fear. I dialed the Sea Horse and asked for Daddy, then handed her the phone. We were standing beside the built-in desk, and I noticed a little cartoon pinned up on the bulletin board next to a picture of my brother with a trophy in his hands. The cartoon was of a woman sitting at a restaurant table, a waiter

standing in front of her. The sign on the window said, "Disillusion-
ment Cafe." The waiter said to the waiting woman, "Your order is not
ready, nor will it ever be." I don't know why but I took the picture of
my brother and slipped it into my pocket.

My mother was screaming into the phone, "You better get here
quick! He's knocking down the house! We'll all be dead! Hurry!"

I went back to stand at the bashed-in wall at the end of the house
to see what progress my brother had made. In the time we were on the
phone he had changed the shape of the pond, knocked down the
gazebo, pulverized the lawn, the carefully laid brick walks that circled
the house, and was starting on the sun room, putting the bulldozer in
reverse to get a good running start.

"What are we going to do? What are we going to do?" My
mother asked the question over and over, until it created a feeling of
hysteria deep within me, and I knew that's what it felt like to be her.

I walked outside to get a better look. He knocked the garage
down with one push as if it were made of tinker toys, then he carried
the debris with the bucket of the bulldozer toward the pond, dumped
it in. On the way back he knocked down a weeping willow tree and
as it fell into the creek I thought of a falling body.

He ground the gears again and turned the machine around and
was coming back toward the front of the house. He ripped out two
more rose bushes, dumped them into the well, and then turned the
bulldozer in a circle, almost gracefully, and headed straight for us.

I called his name. "Morgan!" I wasn't sure if he could hear me
over the screaming of the machine. The bulldozer kept coming toward us. I put my hands around my mouth and called his name again.
"*Mor-gan!*" But I made no move toward him.

My father came driving up the gravel road at a hundred miles an
hour. The car spun sideways to the edge of the circular driveway when

he slammed on the brakes. He got out, leaving the door open, the music blaring.

"God damn son of a bitch what the hell do you think you're doing you crazy bastard this is where we live?" His face was beet red and his hands were trembling.

The bulldozer was about thirty yards away, at the edge of the creek, and it was moving toward the house, toward the picture window, in front of which stood my mother and me, and now my father.

I looked from my mother to my father. We looked at each other, helpless. We didn't even know what.

"And now here's one for you Willie Nelson fans!"

My father went inside the house and came out with the shotgun he kept on a gunrack above the mantel in the family room.

By this time the bulldozer was moving up the front walk, scraping up the cleanly laid bricks as it came.

"Stop." My father said it once. The vein was standing out in his forehead. His face was getting redder and his hands were still trembling and he looked like a wild animal and the next time he said it—"Stop!"—I could smell the whiskey on his breath.

My brother yelled, "You are no longer my father," and kept coming, and I made no move to stand between them. He raised the bucket on the bulldozer and my father raised his rifle. My father said it again—"Stop!"—and then looked at us puzzled, as if this weren't the way it was supposed to go, as if someone had been thrown from a window and had drifted upward instead of falling.

When my brother was less than twenty feet away my father shot him, and my brother grabbed his thigh with his right hand, but the machine kept coming.

"No!" my mother screamed, "No! No! No!" and then she fainted and my father dropped the gun and looked at it as if it were alive and said, "Oh my God, oh my God," a man who had never prayed in his life.

I picked up the gun and jammed it against my shoulder, and squinted my left eye. The day went black. I moved the gun to my left shoulder and got him in my sight. The gun felt awkward in my arms, using my left eye unnatural, but I cocked it and moved the cartridge forward.

"Stop!" I yelled. "Stop or I'll shoot!"

My brother laughed his crazy laugh and the bulldozer kept coming, crashing into the bricks while my father and I stumbled backward, trying to get out of the way.

I don't remember the gun going off, though I do remember pulling the trigger. He fell from the high seat of the bulldozer in slow motion, but the bulldozer kept coming, as if it had a will of its own.

"Sarah!" my father yelled, "Sarah, look out!"

I scrambled up on the moving bulldozer and shut it down, the teeth of the bucket halfway through the big-screen TV that stood inside the picture window. It looked like a caterpillar caught in the midst of transformation.

It was suddenly quiet, except for some lonely music still coming from Daddy's car.

I sat there on the high seat and looked down at my mother lying on the ground, my father kneeling beside my brother, feeling for a pulse, his lips moving but no sound coming out, my brother lying very still. Dead. It's a word you can't really get your mind around. Your brother, dead. And you did it.

Any night now they will be calling from the Freak and Grief Show. How does it feel to be a one-eyed woman and to shoot your brother, your brother who is destroying your parents' home, everything they have spent their lives working for, the grape arbor, the rose garden, the pond, the weeping willows, even the oak tree that has stood over a hundred years? I have my answer ready: Bad. Who is responsible? The question is more difficult.

When the police came this time I knew what it was for. Six officers in three black-and-whites. I don't know why they would send six officers for a woman my size.

They were very polite and spoke in soft voices and they didn't shove me up against the hood, which struck me as odd.

They put my brother in a body bag and looked at him with sympathy because, even if they hated him when he was alive, death is a kind of exemption.

Before they zipped it up, I knelt down and held my brother's face in my hands and wept. I loved him more dead than alive. I was ashamed at how much I loved him. I closed his eyes. Joe Buck did that for Ratso Rizzo in *Midnight Cowboy. Rico*, he'd insisted. *When we get to Florida, call me Rico.* But he never made it. Joe Buck closed Rico's eyes when he died on the bus to Florida. Sat there in the seat beside Rico with his arm around his shoulder, protecting him from the ugly curiosity of on-lookers, from the superiority of the living toward the dead, as if death were a huge insult and love alone was an adequate response to it.

"We'll have to ask you a few questions, Sir."

Again I saw my father's lips move but I didn't hear what was being said.

When they asked me what had happened, I told them. The officers looked from one to the other but I couldn't read their expressions.

One officer, the shortest one, said he'd like to speak with my mother. We all looked down at the ground where she had fallen.

"There she is," I said. For some reason this struck me as funny and I couldn't stop laughing.

My father and one of the officers carried my mother into the house. I followed them down the hall, and when I got to the end, where their bedroom was, I caught a glimpse of myself in the full-length mirror, and I stood there staring, trying to understand what had happened, what I'd become.

They laid my mother on the bed, and loosened the top two buttons of her blouse. "I'm sorry, Sir," the officer said, and I thought his voice held grief.

When my mother came to, she said to my father, "I'd rather he'd killed us all than to see you do what you did. I'll never be able to get it out of my head." Apparently she'd fainted before I shot him. Even after she knew the truth she blamed my father. I understood then that the blame had come first.

My father didn't protest his innocence; he nodded and got up, left the room, walked slowly down the hall, out the front door, and got into the back of a police car.

When I came out the front door, one of the officers put handcuffs on my wrists, as if I might not come willingly. But then he held the door open for me, a high school date, and put his hand on the top of my hair so I wouldn't hurt my head, and it seemed a gesture of kindness.

"Hi, honey," my father said, like this was normal, father and daughter, riding together in a police car.

Out the back window I watched the other two black cars follow us all the way to the end of the gravel road, and only once did I think of the bars of gold inside the black safe, all neatly stacked up on every shelf, and only once did I whisper the combination under my breath, "Seven, twenty-one, seven, left, right, left."

THIS IS A PICTURE OF ME IN THREE
unflattering poses. Right profile. Left. Face forward. They wouldn't
let me comb my hair, which is normally my best feature. These are my
fingerprints below. Before putting me in the cell, I was strip-searched,
an experience I am unlikely to forget, being treated like a piece of
meat, as if I had no inner life, no feelings that might deserve protection from assault, the eyes of strangers.

I gave the bail bondswoman the two-carat diamond ring as my
ten percent on the hundred thousand that was set for my bail, and she
said, "It's all right with me, sweetie, if you never come back." It didn't
seem like stealing. More like a loan. Arlene won't miss it. The trial
will not begin until February at the earliest, maybe March. With any
luck I will be free for another spring, to see the wheat high in the sun,
the blossoms on the almond trees, little pockets of light.

My attorney's name is Deidre Blair. Her first official act after
hearing my story was to call in my psychiatrist for a consultation. Dr.
Glass came right away, in a pale gray suit the exact color of her eyes.
As soon as Ms. Blair heard the word Prozac, her face lit up like it was
Christmas, which it almost was.

When she made her first proposal I shook my head.

"Unless you have a plea called Temporary Sanity, I pass."

She tried another tack. What about self-defense? Did you believe your life was in danger?

"No more than usual."

Did you believe there was nothing else you could do, no other way out?

"I could have moved away," I said. "But this was my home."

They talked until their voices were hoarse, reciting facts, words like *reasonable doubt,* what the jury might think, the likely consequences, my probable regret, and I thought of Angela holding her breath, her cheeks puffing out, her refusal to see the truth even if it meant unconsciousness, early death.

"A person should claim what's hers."

Were you protecting your family? Didn't you believe their lives were threatened? He was driving that bulldozer straight at you, after all, your mother had fainted, your father was crying, your grandmother just buried.

I said, very quietly, as close to certainty as I would come, "Let me tell you what happened." Then I repeated the few facts I had, the beliefs I was unwilling to give up, the possible shape they made in the dark. I told the story again and again, until I saw in their faces acquiescence if not understanding. I killed him. Not because of the Prozac; the Prozac only gave me confidence. Not for Arlene or for my mother, for the destruction of her roses. Not even for the sake of our family, what was left of it. I did it for Jake, for Uncle Ad, for anyone at the mercy of a larger hand, for me.

6:45. ANGELA WILL BE HERE SOON.
I make a batch of Ramos Fizzes in the blender, then straighten up in
the living room, fluff the pillows, pick the lint from the wool rug.
Now that I know I'm leaving, the place looks different, more precious, like a picture of someone you know will die later that day.

I wrap the wedding picture of Rich and me in leftover Christmas
paper and put it in a small box, ready to mail. I wonder where he is
right now, if he thinks of me, whether his second wife has become, by
long habit, his real wife. He has been married to her now almost as
long as he was married to me.

I want my past back. But this is probably bad faith, or good faith
but only for an hour. Already the desire is altered by doubt.

There was a moment when I understood that we would not be
together, even in the indistinct future where hope had its way, even if
it was what we both wanted. It came in a short silence during his last
telephone call, on Christmas Eve, the night Angela brought me home.

"You'll always be the real love of my life," he said, "but when it
comes to the nut-cuttin', I just couldn't do it."

I already knew it. True love renounces everything, even goodness, and this he could not do and be the man I loved. A paradox. Like
my eye he was gone for good. All suffering would not be redeemed.

The lightbulb theory of truth is out, along with the garbage theory of dreams. There is just enough sense to make you doubt it, just enough truth for that doubt to fester and make a sore of your disbelief. *Life isn't easy. Love never lasts.* Even these small consolations are denied us. Love sometimes survives, but beyond recognition, not meeting any present need. Life is so easy some days you don't see the crack widening between your feet.

I have to be out of here by the second. Day after tomorrow. I haven't decided yet where I'll live until the trial begins. But Ted has promised me my job back. I'm willing now to wear a patch over my eye in order to work, a compromise with reality that some would call moral progress. Perhaps one day I will even consent to plastic surgery and have the doctor insert a glass eye. I've been told that if it's done by an artist, it's hard to tell the difference. From the outside, that is.

One thing I do know: I won't be spending my days on the beach in Carmel. I couldn't take the gold. I tried to picture myself sneaking into the house of the dead, pale fingers on the dial of the shiny black safe, heart beating hard, a lump in my throat that wouldn't pass, seven, twenty-one, seven, left, right, left, lifting the bricks out, one by one, into a wheelbarrow, perhaps, my wrists weak, my upper lip beaded with sweat. If I took the gold, I could buy this place from Mom and Daddy, live here forever when I got out of prison. If they ever wanted to come home, it would be here, waiting. If not, I could leave it to Morgan's sons, and to Sunny. Three houses, one for each. His sons would be better off for my greed. It wouldn't do Morgan any good now, would it? Nothing would be served by leaving it in the safe, except Leona Marie's interests, and the gold wasn't hers, she didn't love Morgan, she didn't even think of him as human. Everything would be served by taking it. I could singlehandedly support Amnesty International. I could endow mental hospitals, universities. And I wouldn't need a job ever again, the loss of my eye wouldn't matter so much. Instead of doing shit jobs in order to eat, I could devote my life, what was left of it, to my real calling, to my art.

"Add it up," I heard Grandfather Blight say.

But then I heard Morgan's voice. "You're the only one I can trust." I heard his voice as vividly as if he had just spoken, and I thought then of the memory we shared, Morgan and I, of Uncle Ad's funeral, of the details we could name, when neither of us had been there—the way the room looked, with the casket in front, the indigo and red of the stained glass window, Jesus on the cross, a halo of thorns on his head, the wreath of carnations that hung on a wooden frame like an easel, the way they slid in a half circle toward the casket after the minister finished his sermon, the old woman in a purple dress with a shaky voice who sang "Nearer My God to Thee" and "The Old Rugged Cross" and "Shepherd Show Me How to Go," what his face looked like, powdery and white, though neither of us had seen a dead person's face, the short clean fingernails, though Uncle Addison's fingernails were never clean because he worked in the garage nearly every night. And I thought I understood now how that was possible: We loved him, and love is a kind of knowledge.

I hear a knock at the door. I peer out the front window, but no one is there, then I see my face in the mirror the family room window has made of the dark, and kick up my right leg, fling my arms into the air, a ritual now whenever I see myself coming. It is a gesture both ludicrous and moving, a half inch of triumph destined for breathtaking defeat. I see Great Grandmother Blight looking back at me across the years, my face reflected in that glass, and in that mutual recognition I will make my provisional home.

I look at the videotape on the end table. *Arlene.* My eyes are drawn to it against my will, as to an automobile accident. But although I know what purpose would be served by watching it, I don't know what would be lost.

Last night my mother called to say that the people who bought the land on the other side of the creek have painted her red brick house white, the beams in front of it black. As if I could not see it from here. "To make it look like a Spanish hacienda, I suppose, but it is *not* a success." The disapproval in her voice is deep. They raise greyhounds, for the dog races that have become popular in southern California. The deal with the Asian businessmen fell through because of something to do with water rights, and these are the people who will live here now. A man and a woman. People who do not see the reason or beauty of brick. Or maybe they do but care more for their vision of what the place could be. They have dug up the old brick path out to the white fig trees and the pomegranates and put in cement, a piece of sidewalk from a mislaid part of the city. They have cut down the weeping willows that ran alongside the creek. Where are they from? The circular driveway too has been cast in concrete, because, the husband said, his wife didn't want to ruin her high heels going from the house to the car.

Today in the *Chronicle* I read, "1991 Gun Deaths Top Auto Fatalities in Texas." The triumph of free will over accidents.

My mother no longer talks of my father, but you can see the loss in her unconscious gestures—as she turns to tell him something that makes her laugh on TV, as she waits to have her cigarette lit and, stumbling over grief, remembers, lights it herself.

My father said, last Tuesday night at the Sea Horse, "Just let them pay interest for ten years. If they don't come up with the money, it's still mine. If they'd done it my way, I'd still own that land in ten years." He is stuck in the past and cannot forgive himself for what he has agreed to, for what he has done of his own free will. It's not coercion that bothers us. I tell him, Let it go. Forgive yourself.

Is what I have done forgivable? Or Morgan? I'm still not certain he did it. But what is knowledge except the best story we can tell, with the few facts we have, what we are unwilling to give up? And even if he didn't do it, he could have. It would have been an act he was proud of, would have laughed over, the image of Arlene bound and gagged and stuffed in a garbage can. This is the brutal side of loyalty.

But a horror story is easier to tell than the truth: how love is mixed up in every evil thing. My brother had loved Arlene and when she betrayed him he'd wanted something in the world to match the way he felt, the way Aunt Martha set the house on fire when Uncle Ad killed himself, the way I got my eye put out. Is such wild grief evil? Even that seems optimistic. Evil too is a kind of order.

I glance again at the video on the end table and imagine the last time I saw him, what it would look like on film, the cloud of dust at the end of the road, the bulldozer moving toward us, beloved.

My brother of course would not look at it this way. He'd begin with Arlene. If only we could fix the first betrayal. If only we knew how to shoot it, how to cut the frame.

Was there another way out? If there was, I couldn't see it. If my mother could have walked out the front door and kept walking, instead of calling Daddy to come home from the bar? If Daddy hadn't been drunk? If I hadn't betrayed my brother in my heart, and then again in my imagination, and so had no right to stand between them? If my sister had been there, to hold her breath, to pray?

I blame us all. Because, of the choices available, it seems most honorable. What would it mean not to blame us? What kind of animals or objects would we have to be? How insignificant the loss?

Our family is dead, not in the ordinary way of not breathing, continuing to be, but in the extraordinary way a loved person lives in the memory, my ex-husband, for instance, his soul intact, moved by a single passion, uncorrupted by circumstance.

I wanted to hate my brother because it would be easier; if absolute loyalty isn't possible, let's have renunciation at least: *You are no longer my* . . . I mouthed the words in front of his grave, made my face cold and implacable, but I couldn't say it. My loyalty is partial and conditional and I am not the person I thought. But even where absolute loyalty isn't possible, there might be love. Love for the part of him that could laugh in the gas chamber. Love for the memory of that day when my leg was caught in the stanchion and it bled and I was horrified by the sight of it and he held my hand and said, "It will be all right."

Again I study the flat black case, this time as if it were a film my brother had made, a film that caught the essence of life as he saw it. What would it mean to watch it? What would it mean if I couldn't, chose not to?

My father, it appears, has taken up permanent residence at the Golddust Inn, with day trips to the Sea Horse across the street to confer with William the First, the bartender. When I want to talk to Daddy, I call King William and have him tell Daddy to call me back on the pay phone. This morning when I talked to him he said he was planning to take that trip to the bottom of the Grand Canyon on a donkey, as soon as the weather warmed up.

"I hope mine's not a stumble bum," he said, having already imagined it fully. "I hope I don't get a donkey whose number's up." Sometimes I think a vivid imagination is a curse, allowing us to see too clearly what is what.

"What about your films?" I asked him. "What about Terrence Malick?"

"Hell, honey," he said, "he only made two films in his whole life.

I guess that puts me two behind him."

If this is an explanation I don't get the point. Then he makes it. "After three drinks," he says, "I stop counting."

My mother's life hasn't changed much. She lives in a little stucco house on South Lombardo and orders her groceries in instead of having my dad bring them. Old age, or perhaps my father's absence, seems to have lifted her depression. Or maybe it's this: when the worst happens, the panic subsides. Yesterday I caught her reading the Bible, the one Grandmother Blight used to read The Daily Lesson from, the one with all the blue chalk markings. I didn't ask whether it was for truth or solace.

I look at my watch. Five after seven. Angela is late. That's one thing in life you can count on.

A month ago, when everything began to come together—the land up for sale, the death of our brother, the end of life as we knew it—and Angela was more melancholy than usual, I told her about the drugs I'm taking, my transformation. She had already seen the evidence with her own eyes, but she didn't know what to attribute it to, this radical change.

"I knew you were different," she said, "that night I could hear the eleven o'clock news because for once you didn't cry all the way through it."

We went to see Dr. Glass together and now she takes the drugs too. The results have been encouraging. As a by-product her ulcer is healing, and her husband's vocal hatred of the world and its inhabitants no longer gives her migraines. She doesn't need Ben and Jerry's Chocolate Fudge Brownie to get through the day. Like me she sleeps nine hours a night. The last cartoon she drew was of Marjorie Morningstar peering over the edge of a cliff, a question mark in the cloud above her head, having forgotten what she came for, a scar like lightning across her forehead. The caption reads, "Little Marjorie, happy at last." We both had a laugh over that.

This time when I suggested she collect her drawings into a book, she didn't protest. We are already planning the publication party. On the royalties, she has promised to take care of me in my old age, if I'm out of jail by then. We will go to live on the sea in Ireland, where our ancestors are from. We will take no guns. She will stop the war between the Catholics and the Protestants through nonviolent means. I will take photographs of faces that tell me something I can use, or who at least know how to keep their mouths shut.

"Unless the money runs out," she said. "Unless we both become bag ladies." We joked about how mine would be a plain and simple brown bag with only the necessities in it: a blanket, a loaf of bread, a book of photographs. Hers would be elaborately decorated, covered with amazing doodads in bright colors with piping and rick-rack along the edges. Inside would be luxuries: small perfumed soaps in the shapes of flowers, lace handkerchiefs to hand out to the needy, white candles for saying novenas, a silver friendship ring like the one she bought for me in Dublin with two hands circling a crown above a heart. My birthday isn't until tomorrow, but she said she couldn't wait, and gave it to me at Christmas. Even if she can't help being good, I love her.

I put my brother's videotape into the VCR and turn it on, then I push the EJECT button. If the truth is vicious, is it virtue to see it? What purpose would it serve except self-justification?

Today I got a letter from my son, postmarked Rouen. His plans have changed. He said he misses some things about the States—bookstores open all night, people who get his jokes, Lucy—and will be coming home earlier than he thought. In closing, as usual, he tells me a story, this one titled "They Don't Know What Love Is." He is work-

ing illegally in a cafeteria, as a dishwasher, and that night he was working late, rubbing the aluminum counters until they shone. The old
dishwasher who speaks English came in. His father had died, and his
eighty-nine-year-old mother didn't understand why he wouldn't
come to the funeral. "He's your father," she said. "I'd rather remember
him the way he was," he told her. "You've got to be careful about the
pictures you put in your head." That's when Sunny confessed that he
had not spoken to his own father in almost a year. It began with a fight
about drinking and firewood and a short silence that continued. The
dishwasher was quiet for a while. "Well, like my father used to say . . ."
The dishwasher stared off into the distance as if he were seeing something just beyond the edge of the picture. He cocked his head, listening. By this time Sunny expected something profound, something to
write down in his book of quotations. "What?" he finally asked, irritated. The dishwasher smiled and shrugged. He said, "'I don't know—
Maybe *I'm* the asshole.'"

For the first time I can recall he did not sign off with "The world
is ugly, and the people are sad." He signed it, "Love, Sunny." And
added, "P.S. Thanks for the video, Mom."

I sent him *Lawrence of Arabia* for his twenty-first birthday last
month, a film in which I thought he might see himself. The scene I
like best is where he lights a match and, without flinching, puts it out
with his thumb and forefinger. William Potter tries it, burns himself,
and yells, "It damn well hurts!" Certainly it hurts, Lawrence replies.
"Then what's the trick?" Potter asks. "The trick," Lawrence says, "is
not to mind that it hurts." Then the lit match turns into the sun rising
on the desert.

I dump the melted batch of Ramos Fizzes down the sink, put
some ice from the freezer in a bowl next to the blender, to have it
ready for a new batch, fluff up the pillows again, stare at the carpet,

searching for lint, dust the large blank projection screen with the back of my forearm, moving my arm in large circles. I am anxious to begin.

The doorbell rings and I go to answer it. Angela is dressed all in white, and I think of the thirteen virgins and the candlelight vigil she held when President Kennedy died. I hug her hard.

"The projection screen is all set up," I say. "I'll get the Ramos Fizzes." Though I've lost my talent for drinking, we have promised each other to carry on this one tradition: Ramos Fizzes, watching home movies at the end of the year, trying to make sense of it.

While I go to start the blender and get the champagne glasses, I hand her something to look at, an eight-by-ten print I made yesterday, of a shopping cart abandoned on the beach at Pacifica. It's my first photograph of the natural world.

She calls out from the living room, "What does it mean?"

I don't know how to answer.

"Maybe something simple, easy to understand? If you shop for groceries at the beach, your basket will be empty?" I can hear her laughter over the screaming of the machine.

Speaking of groceries, I saw Jake in the Safeway on Mariposa Road last Sunday. He was with a very tiny person with a narrow face and eyes like a ferret. He told her to go ahead and he would catch up. He called her Grace. It's insulting what a man will take up with when you're no longer in the picture.

"Some kind of friend you turned out to be," he said, smiling.

For a minute I didn't get it. And then I did, a kind of double irony, and I had to congratulate him—on his talent for seeing the world through his own eyes.

Who is better off? Him with no illusions about loyalty to be lost? Or me? Consider a series of photographs. If it started here, with two eyes and bright promise, the photograph with one eye missing would be a loss. If it started with both eyes gone, however, and went to one.

I carry the blender and the champagne glasses into the family room, set them on the coffee table, pour one for Angela, one for me.

We sit together on the couch, my sister and I, under the rose comforter, the comforter we made a tent of when we were children, laying it over the card table on the lawn, crawling inside, hiding in the dark, hoping to be found. We clink our glasses together and speak in quiet tones about the fact that we will never again all be in the same room at the same time. Members of a new race, we must learn to breathe the harsh air.

"Shall we get started?" Angela asks.

We are skipping the whipped cream and strawberry waffles this year because Angela is on a diet. She's given up sugar. In the last three weeks she has lost seven pounds without guilt, even though she believes that somewhere in Argentina or Australia another woman's hips are widening. For Angela, such selfishness is progress.

And what about me? I've given up serious drinking, self-pity, the grief that was Jake, my ex-husband, trash TV, the luxury of refusing an eye patch, unemployment. What's left?

I turn on the projector, adjust the focus, go back and settle on the couch, take my sister's hand in mine, noticing the darkening spots that mar her perfect skin. Then the moving shadows start and, two children at a matinee, we snuggle under the comforter and watch as the room goes dark, the lights come on, and all of us in our Thanksgiving best—our father, mother, Morgan, Angela, me, Uncle Ad sitting beside Aunt Martha in the cockpit of his Cessna, children of every age and size, Uncle Bertie free on bail, Grandfather Blight in his green Northern Pacific uniform, Grandmother Blight showing off her gold nugget ring, Richard, when we were married, and Sunny smiling, even my mother's parents are there, she with the squirrel-faced fur around her neck, he with the felt-gray Stetson and one gold front tooth, and there's my great grandmother in a long red dress, one leg flung up so high it threatens her ear, her arms raised in defiance, her skirts flying—come to life.

&